The Cappuccino Collection

By

Kay Seeley

ISBN:978-0-9933394-1-7
ISBN:

To: Magazine readers everywhere,

without whom there would be no stories.

Author's Note

All the stories in *The Cappuccino Collection*, except one, have been previously published in magazines, anthologies or on the internet. There are romantic, humorous and thought provoking stories of real life, love and the ties that bind, to be enjoyed in small bites.

If this collection were a cake it would be a deeply satisfying Chocolate Gateau

Please feel free to contact Kay through her website www.kayseeleyauthor.com

She'd love to hear from you.

CONTENTS

Brief Encounter

What a day, Katie thought as she packed up and left the office. First the photocopier had chewed up the document she was working on, then her friend Penny had rung to cancel the after-work girls' night out they had planned and to cap it all the incessant rain had turned into a full blown storm. At least it was the end of the week and she had the weekend to look forward to.

Blasted rain, she thought as she dashed to the bus stop. A fresh torrent lashed against the shop windows. She dived into a doorway for cover and collided with a man already sheltering there.

"Oh, sorry," she said. "I didn't see you."

"No problem," he said, moving over to make room for her.

"Thanks." She glanced out. "Cats and dogs weather my gran used to call it, though God knows why, it's not fit for either."

She saw the corners of his mouth curve into an 'almost' smile. Blue eyes twinkled beneath his floppy blonde hair.

"Are you waiting for the bus too?" she asked.

"Me? No, going to the station to get a train, although…" he raised his arm to check his watch, a heavy gold one, "looks as though I've probably missed it."

Katie sighed. Would this rain never stop? "Got far to go?" she asked - anything to relieve the boredom of what promised to be a long, wet wait.

"Spangler's Mead. Don't suppose you've ever heard of it. It's a small village out of town." His voice was cultured, or cut glass as Katie called it. Upper class anyway. She smiled at the incongruity of it. He sounded like he was more used to chauffeur driven Bentleys than bus stops.

She frowned. "Spangler's Mead! That's where I live. I get the bus. It takes longer but it's cheaper." She stared at him, trying to place his face. He was younger than her but she was surprised she didn't recognise him. "It's a wonder I haven't seen you in the village. Place is smaller than a postage stamp. I thought I knew everyone. What's your name?"

"Clive."

"I'm Katie, how do you do?" She extended her hand. Now he'll think I'm trying to pick him up, she thought. "Have you lived there long?"

"All my life."

"Me too. I went to the local school. You?"

"'Fraid not."

No, Katie thought, posh public school I bet. Still, talking to him helped pass the time and, if she was honest, it was the nicest thing that had happened to her today. "Well you must know some people in the village," she said.

"Err…um…well. I guess I know the woman who runs the post office. Ghastly woman, quite beastly. Keeps everyone waiting while she gossips with the old dears collecting their pensions. Never has a good word to say about anybody. Miserable old baggage."

"The postmistress, Gladys?" Katie said. "She's my aunt."

2

It was difficult to see in the shadow but Katie thought she felt the heat from his reddening face as he shuffled his feet in his shiny, rain-spattered shoes. "Oh sorry. Didn't mean…" but it was too late; his words were out and couldn't be sucked back. He looked as though he wanted to melt into the floor.

Katie laughed. "She's not really. I was joking, but you should see your face." She jumped as thunder cracked overhead, lightening flashed and a fresh onslaught of rain lashed against the windows. "So, what do you do for living? Anything interesting?"

He grimaced. "I work in the bank."

"Oh, a banker. Shouldn't you have a bowler hat and an umbrella?"

"Well, yes. I do actually, but we only wear them on ceremonial occasions, along with the pinstriped trousers and frock coat. What about you?"

She immediately warmed to him. "I never wear a bowler hat, nor a frock coat. I work in a solicitor's office." She glanced out at the rain. "An umbrella would be handy. Then you wouldn't have to shelter in shop doorways with the hoi polloi."

"Don't you have one in that portmanteau of a bag you're carrying? My mother never goes anywhere without an umbrella. Says you can't trust the British weather."

"Pity she's not here then isn't it?"

Another clap of thunder and burst of lightening rent the sky. Katie banged her hands together and stamped her feet. Her gloves did nothing to keep her hands warm, her shoulder-length chestnut hair was beginning to frizz and her nose was turning blue. She noticed his good quality overcoat and wished she had worn something warmer.

"It doesn't look like it's going to let up any time soon," he said, gazing out. "There's a café down the road.

Do you fancy a coffee? At least it'll be dry and warm inside."

Katie smiled, she had nothing else to do, nothing to rush home for. What the hell, she thought. "Good idea," she said. "Let's make a run for it."

Inside the café, the windows drizzled condensation, but the warming smell of coffee and cake filled the air. Katie breathed it in, glad to be in the dry. She glanced around at the dark wood and soft amber lighting. It looked cosy and inviting. Clive shook the rain from his coat. "You find a table and I'll get the coffee. What'll it be?"

She gazed up at the menu. Should she go for cappuccino, or something more exotic? He moved impatiently from foot to foot, almost huffing but not quite.

"Cappuccino please," she said eventually.

She found a table at the back, peeled off her gloves, took off her coat and shook the rain from it. The café was warm and the seat comfortable; a definite improvement on the shop doorway. She rubbed her hands together, suddenly conscious of the ring sparkling on her finger.

He arrived with the coffee and she embraced the cup with her hands to warm them. "So, how old are you and what made you take up banking?"

"Twenty-three and my father. You?"

"Twenty-nine and hoping to marry a rich solicitor before I'm thirty."

"And will you?"

She wiggled her finger; the diamonds sparkled in the light. "Half-way there already," she said. She sipped her coffee and beamed him a mischievous grin. He looked like a fun guy, unlike her fiancé, Richard, who wore his gravitas like an all-enveloping shield. "So, what would you be doing if your father hadn't made you go into the bank?"

"Er…um…well… Something creative I suppose. In my spare time I… No, you'll laugh."

"No I won't." She looked serious. "Everyone has a dream, what's yours?"

He shook his head. "Promise you won't laugh."

"I promise." Katie crossed her heart.

He swallowed a gulp of coffee. "I can't believe I'm telling you this," he said. "In my spare time I design t-shirts. You know, front and back: logos, slogans, pictures." His eyes shone with excitement as he spoke. "Some are really quite good."

"So – why don't you do it professionally, if that's what you want?"

He sighed. "My father would go ballistic if he knew. It's my secret vice – designing t-shirts." He held his head in his hands. "Pathetic aren't I?"

"No, you're not. I think it's great. Listen, I have a sister…" She saw sudden fear on his face. "No not that. She's at Art College doing Textiles and Design. She could print out your designs and sell them in the market along with hers. It'd be great."

Clive looked aghast. "Good heavens, no. I could never do that, not in a million years. My father'd have my guts for garters."

"So, bankers wear garters do they? I always suspected they did." She giggled. "And made of guts – wouldn't surprise me. Seriously though, you should follow your dream. You never know what's around the corner."

As she said it, Katie recalled how her world had been turned upside down five years ago when both her parents died within months of each other and she'd been left to look after her sister, Zizzi. She adored Zizzi beyond reason. They'd helped each other through the bad times and clung together like limpets tossed on a stormy sea. But now she worried about her; she was wild and unpredictable. Crazy as only teenagers finding their feet can be. She was always pushing boundaries and Katie worried that one day she'd push too far.

Clive gazed out of the window. Katie noticed the dreamy faraway look in his eyes but said nothing. The rain had subsided to a steady downpour.

He smiled at her. "Look, instead of the train or the bus why don't we share a taxi? It won't cost much more than the train fare."

Katie's eyes widened. "You'll never get a taxi on a Friday night in the rain. They all hibernate you know – most of them won't come out again until spring."

Clive grinned, took out his mobile phone and pressed a couple of buttons. "Clive Barrington-Smythe here. I need a pick-up ASAP at…" he picked up the café menu, "The Copper Pot, 16 High Street... Yes… ten minutes…fine."

"Wow. A taxi firm on speed dial. I'm impressed."

In the taxi, Katie insisted on paying her share although Clive said it didn't matter.

"No. I insist. After all, you got the coffee." She dived into her bag and rummaged around. After a few moments of burrowing through the bag's contents, she said, "Sorry. I've forgotten my purse. Must have left it at work. Give me your address and I'll pop the money round in the morning."

"There's really no need," he said.

"I insist."

Clive shrugged, wrote his address on a piece of paper and handed it to her. Her eyebrows rose. "Daddy owns the bank then?" she said.

When they arrived in Spangler's Mead Katie said, "You can drop me off at the post office." She chuckled when she saw the look of horror on his face. "It's okay," she said. "She's not my aunt, I live around the corner." She got out of the taxi and waved the paper in the air. "I'll drop the cash round in the morning."

The next morning Clive was in the kitchen when the doorbell rang. His father was in his study and his mother in the garden. "I'll get it," he called hurrying to the door. He almost choked when he opened it. A girl, dressed in purple striped leggings, the shortest skirt on record and a jacket that would put Joseph's Technicolor Dreamcoat to shame, stood on the doorstep. His pulses raced. Orange and yellow feathers stuck out of the knot of rainbow coloured hair on top of her head. Blue and green tendrils framed a face pale as an angel's wing. Zing went his heart-strings. He could hardly breathe.

"Hi," she said. "I'm Zizzi, Katie's sister." Her eyes, outlined in iridescent indigo, held the promise of pleasures unknown. "She asked me to give you this." She pulled an envelope out of her gold-fringed bag. He noticed her violet nails, painted to match her lipstick. He stared.

"Can I use your khasi?" she said. "I'm dying for a pee."

Stunned, he opened the door wider to let her in.

"Katie said there'd be a chance of coffee an' all."

Clive swallowed. It took all his inner resources to recover himself sufficiently to say, "Yes, yes, of course. How crass of me. Come in. Loo's there, kitchen at the end of the hall. I'll put the coffee on." A broad grin lit up his face.

In the kitchen, he struggled to control his excitement. He filled the coffee maker and switched it on. Wow, he thought, Katie's right, you never know what's around the corner. One thing he did know for sure was that his parents would go BALLISTIC.

First published in Take a Break Fiction Feast in 2013 as Romance in the Rain.

Some Enchanted Evening

Stepping off the plane in Italy felt like walking into a warm caress. Any fear I had about travelling alone evaporated when I saw the tanned, smiling faces that greeted me: so unlike the cold indifference of the people at home.

"I don't know why you want to go gadding about in some foreign country at your age," my neighbour, George had said when I told him about my proposed visit. His mouth twisted into a jellyfish pout as he emphasised the last three words.

"At my age! I'm sixty-two, not one-hundred-and-two," I said, more determined than ever to go. A spur of the moment impulse on a cold winter's day lured me into booking a place on an off-peak, cultural tour of Italy. It promised sunshine in an exotic setting. I'd never been abroad, so I thought it would be an adventure. "It'll be a nice change," I said. "A week away will be just the ticket."

George reached for his tea. "Hmph, you have to watch those Italians. All flash and no substance," he said. He ran a patronising eye over me as he sipped his drink. "Still, you should be all right."

Cheek, I thought, I may be old but I'm not dead. "What a shame," I said. "A holiday romance might spice things up a bit."

George scowled.

The girl in the travel agent's was helpful. "This one includes trips to Florence and Pisa, plus a tour of Tuscany and a visit to a local vineyard," she said, showing me the brochure. "There's an old watermill too and the countryside is stunning."

"Do you think I'll be all right," I asked, "travelling alone at my age?"

She laughed. "To breathe the air of Italy is to stay forever young," she said. She wasn't wrong.

The hotel nestled in the arms of surrounding hills, its pink painted walls a perfect backdrop to balconies brimming with geraniums, begonias and verbena. An abundance of hibiscus and bougainvillaea scented the air and perfectly laid out lawns led from the curving stone terrace steps to a shimmering pool, set like a diamond amid grassy banks. It was everything I could ever have hoped for. My heart soared.

Sunday morning, as I sat in the shade of bright yellow awnings in a café in the square, I fell under Italy's spell. I turned my face to the sun and breathed in the heady fragrance of Madonna lilies. Beneath a sky as blue as the pictures in the brochures. Church bells pealed in the distance and around me the square buzzed with activity. The rise and fall of conversation filled my ears, along with the chink of glasses and the occasional burst of laughter. I gazed at the scene, drinking in the atmosphere. I tried to capture it all in a snapshot of memory to be revisited later, on cold, dark winter nights at home.

I poured three sachets of sugar into the thick, frothy cappuccino, sprinkled with chocolate, in front of me. I chuckled at the memory of what George had said. "You'll be drinking that cost-a-fortune frothy coffee stuff next," he said. "Arty-farty nonsense. Nothing like a good old fashioned cup of tea." George wouldn't understand how indulgent the coffee made me feel, but he was right about something. It doesn't matter where you are, if you're sitting alone in a cafe, you're sitting alone. The relaxed fellowship of the people around me seemed to highlight my isolation.

By Wednesday, I'd been jostled by the crowds in Pisa, charmed by the medieval beauty of San Gimignano and overawed by the grandeur of the Campo in Sienna. I'd thrilled to the magnificence of the churches, the weight of history in the ancient buildings, been enlightened by the culture and overwhelmed by the passion of the people. I'd wandered in olive groves and citrus orchards where soft breezes whispered through leaves and gardens overflowed with life and colour. I'd strolled through crowded markets between stalls piled high with everything from silk scarves to hand-made shoes, all stylish, designer labelled and unbelievable cheap. I loved it.

So many wonderful things to see, I thought, what a pity I've no one to share them with. George doesn't know what he's missing. I'd gained so much in such a short time, my awareness and outlook on life had somehow been lifted to a higher level of consciousness.

Thursday morning there was a coach trip to a local vineyard, followed by lunch at a trattoria and then on to the citrus orchards. At the vineyard, I sampled the wine generously; at lunch I enjoyed a glass or two of Chianti and later found the Limoncello worthy of trying several glasses. By the time we got back to the hotel I felt satisfyingly euphoric and quite reckless. The rest of the group had returned to their rooms, so I sat by myself on the terrace and ordered a glass of cool, crisp Prosecco in place of my usual afternoon tea. I took out my book. In the background John Lennon's voice floated through the open doors of the hotel bar. I heard him asking where all the lonely people came from. We don't come from anywhere, I thought. We're here all the time, you just haven't noticed. I closed my book and sighed.

I had almost dozed off in the afternoon sunshine when the arrival of a tall, silver-haired man jerked me out of my reverie. Immaculately dressed in pressed chinos and the crispest, pale turquoise shirt I'd ever seen, he came and stood by my table.

"May I join you?" he said. A seductive Italian accent enriched his honey smooth voice. A shiver of pleasure ran down my spine. How come Italian men are all so handsome and well-dressed I thought, immediately picturing Rossano Brazzi in *South Pacific*. I almost expected him to burst into a chorus of *Some Enchanted Evening*. Goose-bumps prickled my body.

"Please do," I said, startled into breathlessness. "To be honest, I'm not very fond of my own company."

He smiled graciously. "The English lady with the ubiquitous book," he said. "You travel alone?"

"Yes, quite alone."

A smile spread across his face as he sat down. "I noticed you at my vineyard this morning. My name is Count Fiorini, but you must call me Phillippe." He held out his hand and when I offered mine, he raised it to his lips. "Charming," he said.

A small bubble of laughter formed in my stomach and grew into a giggle I found hard to suppress. "Maureen," I said, "but you must call me Mo, everyone does. So, it was your vineyard?"

"Yes, and when I saw you this morning I thought your eyes carried a great sadness. In Italy we do not allow beautiful ladies to be alone and to look sad." His eyes gazed intently into mine. My heart fluttered.

"Sad? No, a little distracted maybe."

"Distracted? You didn't enjoy the tour?"

A guilty blush warmed my face, already flushed from the day's intake of alcohol. I remembered thinking that the smell from the winery was worse than George's socks when he slipped his shoes off under my table.

"No, really, I found it most interesting," I lied, and then, and I don't know to this day what made me say it, I added, "Pity it wasn't the villa though. I would have preferred a tour around the villa."

A huge grin lit up his face.

"It will be my pleasure to escort you around my villa," he said, his eyes sparkling like fireworks in the night sky. He stood up and offered me his arm.

It felt like a challenge, so I linked my arm through his and allowed him to lead me to his gleaming silver Mercedes.

The tour of the villa was like walking around Buckingham Palace only much smaller and more intimate. Afterwards, he pointed out that I had missed dinner and insisted I stay and eat with him. We dined on the terrace overlooking the pool. Scented candles filled the air with jasmine and overhead lanterns danced, their reflection like stars on the shimmering water.

We drank Chianti and ate salty sweet prosciutto and succulent melon drizzled with tangy citrus dressing, followed by melt-in-the-mouth spaghetti in a sauce light and fresh as winter sunshine. An orchestra played softly in the background while, around us, the setting sun bathed the Tuscan hills in the sulphur glow of twilight. It was magical, like coming home after a long, arduous journey.

"Thank you for a wonderful dinner," I said.

"It's the least I can do to repay you for such delightful company." His tanned face creased into a mega-watt smile its brilliance only outdone by the sparkle in his cobalt eyes.

I lost track of what I drank, but I felt suitable floaty when he suggested a swim. "I didn't bring my costume," I teased.

"Costumes not required," he said. "It's very private here."

We swam naked watched only by a pale ghost of a moon and a plethora of stars. His muscular, athletic torso and my not so athletic but still trim, white-as-a-statue body, side by side. I couldn't help wondering what George would have said. His disapproval billowed around me like a darkening cloud, but a gentle breeze sighing through the Cypress trees soon wafted it away.

The next day, on the trip to Florence, I decided to forgo the visit to the Uffizi Gallery. Instead, I wandered along the narrow, cobbled streets, browsing the market stalls and staring, unseeing, into the windows of the shops along the Ponte Vecchio. The events of the evening replayed in my mind, like an elusive dream I couldn't quite recapture. Why can't English men be as romantic as Italians, I thought. Next to Phillipe, George looked extremely dull. I valued our friendship, but wished he were a tad more exciting.

I bought George a bottle of Italian Brandy. For myself I bought a postcard of the Villa Fiorina.

At the airport the next day, sitting in the café with a thick, frothy cappuccino, sprinkled with chocolate, I took out my book. Not my *Guide to Tuscany,* but a novel entitled *The Romantic Italian,* the sort of thing George would describe as trashy romantic rubbish, but I thought it somehow appropriate. I heard someone say "Mind if I join you?"

My heart leaped with joyful anticipation. I looked up. It dived rapidly when I recognised the man who'd sat behind me on the coach. I'd overheard him complaining about the Italian war effort and saying that if it hadn't been for Mussolini the trains wouldn't run on time.

"Mind if I join you," he repeated, more slowly and loudly, mouthing the words and waving frantically at the empty chair, as if I was senile. With his sparse grey hair and matching moustache he reminded me of George.

"I'd rather you didn't," I said. "To be honest I'm rather fond of my own company."

Short-listed in the Ponsara Prize Competition and published on the Internet in 2011

Message in a Bottle

Everyone does it, nobody thinks anything of it. Vanessa and Ronnie never thought twice about doing it, it just seemed the right and natural thing to do.

They sat entwined on the shingle beach after celebrating their second wedding anniversary with a picnic of fish and chips. It was a clear moonlit night, warm for the time of year. The heavens were full of stars. A soft spring breeze caressed their faces and ruffled their hair as they watched the boats rock gently on the swell. Above the whooshing of the waves the faint pulse of music drifted across from the pier where neon lights chased patterns in the night sky. Vanessa snuggled up to Ronnie.

They'd finished their fish and chips and two bottles of wine and were feeling quite mellow. The smell of chips and vinegar lingered in the air. Ronnie found some paper and a pen. Vanessa licked the salt from her fingers and wrote:

'Please send more wine.'

She added their address, put the message in one of the bottles, sealed it and Ronnie threw it into the sea. They cheered when they heard the splash in the darkness. Vanessa sighed, but thought no more about it. It was the sort of thing anyone would do.

Several months later the hot summer sun brought crowds to the beach. Ice-cream vendors and deck-chair attendants did a roaring trade. The promenade filled with people walking and the beach with children laughing and playing in the sunshine.

Vanessa was at first puzzled and then amazed when she received a postcard with a picture of the D-Day landings on the front. The message read:

'Your bottle picked up in Normandy.'

There was a date which was smudged so she couldn't quite make it out, but the spidery writing gave a return address in East Anglia.

Vanessa was stunned. She had to take a couple of deep breaths and read the card three times before it sunk in. She remembered throwing the bottle into the sea, the message with her address on it, but had never expected any reply – it was just a joke.

She tried to imagine the fragile glass bottle bobbing all the way across the busiest shipping lanes in the world to arrive safely in France. Not only had the bottle survived but someone had picked it up and read the message – amazing! She was dead excited and showed the card to all her friends. They talked about it for weeks.

Vanessa was so bowled over by her incredible luck she even wrote to the local newspaper. They sent a photographer who took a picture of her and the postcard. In a burst of gratitude to the sender she decided to reply so she bought a nice postcard with a picture of Winchester Cathedral on and wrote:

'Thanks for the card, but where is the wine?'

She thought it funny at the time.

The following week the postman delivered a large cardboard box. It was heavy and Vanessa had to sign for it so she knew it was something special. She almost died when she opened it and found a dozen bottles of wine inside. Not cheap stuff either; there was Shiraz, Merlot, Chardonnay, Pinot Grigio, Cabernet Sauvignon and Rioja. There was no note, no invoice, nothing to say who had sent it. She thought about the postcard, but soon dismissed the idea. She wasn't fool enough to believe anyone would send an expensive box of wine to a stranger just because they'd asked for it. No, someone was having a laugh.

She rang the number on the box.

"I've received this box of wine," she said.

"Yes Madam?"

"Well, I didn't order it. Can you tell me who did and why it's been sent to me?" She gave her name and address and the gentleman on the other end went to check.

"Yes, I can confirm the delivery but I'm afraid I can't give out our customers' details. You'll have to contact them yourself."

"How can I when I don't know who they are?"

"Sorry. Data Protection Act and all that." He put the phone down.

I bet it's Ronnie playing games, she thought. He'd always been a bit of a joker had Ronnie. He'd pulled more strokes than Oxford and Cambridge boat crews put together. Well, Vanessa thought, I'll soon sort him out.

She didn't say anything but that evening she put a clean white cloth on the table and got out their good cutlery and glasses, even though it was only Wednesday and they were just having pie and mash. She opened a bottle of the wine and set it on the table.

When Ronnie came in he called, "Hi, I'm home," then took one look and went out again. He returned about ten minutes later with some yellow and white flowers wrapped in cellophane. "Sorry love, must have forgotten," he said thrusting them at her.

Vanessa took them and sniffed. "Lovely," she said. She could tell he'd got them from the garage on the corner. No smell and a bit straggly but it's the thought that counts. "Forgotten what?" she said.

"I dunno, must be something." He waved his arm at the table. "Wine an' all. What we celebrating?"

"Nothing," she said, "but we've got the wine, might as well drink it."

"Wine?" he said, a puzzled frown on his face. Then he noticed the box on the floor. "Where'd this come from?"

"As if you didn't know," she said.

"No, honest."

Well, she thought, if he wants to play games. "Must have been the chap who sent the postcard," she said. "I must remember to thank him."

"Chap who sent the post-card? You're kidding?"

"Well, if it wasn't you…"

The frown on Ronnie's face deepened. He walked over to the box and inspected it. "Must be some mistake," he said. "Are you sure it's paid for? It's not one of those scams where they send out free samples and you get a huge bill the following week? I don't think we should be drinking it." Ronnie looked genuinely perturbed but he didn't fool Vanessa. She knew him of old. He'd always been a wind up merchant, she wasn't about to fall for one of his tricks again.

"No it's okay," she said. "All above board. I checked. Let's just enjoy it."

Ronnie said he still didn't feel right about it but she'd poured it out by then.

Ronnie kept protesting. "Are you sure?" he said when she opened the second bottle. "I don't feel right about this. Someone must have made a mistake and we'll end up paying for it." He shook his head. "We should send it back."

"Can't," Vanessa said. "We've drunk half of it." She was almost convinced he knew nothing about it – almost.

Ronnie shook his head. For a moment he looked as though he wasn't enjoying it. If she didn't know him better Vanessa might have believed him.

"If you feel so bad why don't we send something in return?" she said. "A couple of bottles of Scotch or some Brandy. My grandfather used to enjoy a nip of brandy before bed."

She never thought Ronnie would go along with it, but he'd had enough alcohol to float a battle ship and by this time he was getting quite broody. He sat quiet for a while deep in thought, or as deep as a man like Ronnie gets. "I'll send a cheque," he said eventually.

"A cheque?"

"Yes, to cover the cost of the wine."

Vanessa thought he was pulling another one of his diabolical strokes but he had a look in his eye that told her not to argue. In fact he was in quite a sulk and it wasn't like Ronnie to mope.

"If you want to drink wine I'll buy you wine," he said, glaring at her. "Anything you need, I'll get it for you. I don't want you accepting expensive gifts from strangers. It's not right. You never know where it might lead." He looked quite fierce. He took a swig of wine, huffed and got up. Vanessa was shocked speechless when he came back with his cheque book and wrote out a cheque for an amount that would have bought twenty bottles of wine.

She gulped back her disbelief, washing it down with a crisp white Chardonnay. Ronnie wasn't joking. So it must have been the man who sent the postcard after all.

Vanessa's face reddened at the thought. How stupid and insensitive she'd been. Of course Ronnie was right. They couldn't accept such a gift from a stranger.

She was afraid their mysterious benefactor might think they'd thrown his gift back in his face, so she wrote a note thanking him for his kindness and hoping he would accept the cheque in the spirit in which it was offered. Ronnie added the cheque and she posted it. Ronnie's display of pique gave her a buzz though. It wasn't often he showed his feelings.

A couple of days later Vanessa was telling her friend Lesley-Anne about it. They were having a girls' night in, settled in front of the TV all geared up to watch a Brad Pitt DVD and knock back several bottles of the good stuff.

"Pass us up a red," she said, pointing to the box on the floor. Lesley leaned over and fished a bottle out of the box. As she did so a card dropped from the bottom of the bottle.

"What's this?" she said, handing it to Vanessa. "It must have slipped down the side of the box."

"Oh my Lord," Vanessa said showing her the card from the local newspaper. It said:

"Congratulations. You have won the prize for this month's most inspiring news item. Please enjoy the enclosed with our compliments.

Vanessa's heart raced. She looked at Lesley-Anne and they both started giggling. "Best not tell Ronnie - ever," she said.

First published in The Weekly News in 2012

To Daddy - Love Amy

Maggie lugged the heavy black bag into the charity shop where she worked two mornings a week. The bag was split and had obviously been riffled through.

"Honest," she said to Ginny who managed the shop. "Stealing from the Hospice – how low can some people get?"

Ginny shrugged. "You have to feel sorry for them if they have to resort to scavenging through our bags," she said. Her brow puckered. "I thought you were off on holiday."

"This afternoon," Maggie said. "I just popped into pick up something to read on the 'plane."

At the bookshelf she picked out a thriller.

"Go on take it – on the house," Ginny said.

"Not likely." Maggie slammed a pound coin on the counter. "That'd be as bad as nicking from the bags outside."

When Maggie and her husband Ken arrived in Spain it felt like walking into a warm embrace. The sun shone in a cloudless sky, colourful swathes of bougainvillea, oleander, poppies and mimosa vied with lilies and lavender to perfume the air. "Now we're here we might as well enjoy ourselves," Maggie said, glaring at her husband Ken.

He grunted. He hadn't wanted to come away. He said they couldn't afford it what with the engineering firm he worked for going bust and taking his pension with it. Every day he'd grown more and more despondent. He'd become tetchy too. Hardly said a word and snapped at her when she made any suggestions. It was only after their Joanna found the 'cheap as chips' holiday to Spain on the internet that Maggie had managed to persuaded him to take the break they both needed. Now she was here she was determined to make the most of it.

The first morning, after breakfast, they wandered into town and had coffee at a small café on the front. Ken read the newspaper and Maggie opened her book.

"Look," she said, showing Ken the book. On the fly-leaf a child's scribble in biro read: '*To Daddy love Amy xxx*'. "Don't you think that's sad?" Maggie said. She couldn't imagine giving away any of her children's gifts. She'd kept all their offerings from the garish primary school paintings to the odd shaped plasticine models they'd produced with such pride. "This must have been somebody's treasured possession once. I wonder how it ended up in the charity shop."

Ken raised an eyebrow. "Not surprising really," he said. "Where do you think all our treasured possessions will go when we pop our clogs? Can't see the kids wanting to keep our stuff. It'll end up on the scrapheap, just like us."

Maggie huffed. He was right. Their children had lives of their own and they'd collect their own treasures to keep their memories alive. Still, she couldn't help feeling sad.

The first day set the pattern for the rest of the holiday. Each morning they'd stroll along to the coffee shop, Ken would read his paper and Maggie her book. In the afternoons, she'd take a dip in the hotel pool and dry off on a sun-bed while her husband enjoyed a spot of male bonding in the local bar watching his beloved football. Gregarious by nature he'd always come back with some tale he'd heard and stories of different people he'd met. He could strike up a conversation in an empty room, unlike Maggie who was content with her own company. Perhaps that's why they got on so well, being so different.

In the evening, after dinner, they'd stroll along the beach hand in hand. Walking in the moonlight, with the sound of the waves lapping the shore, Maggie felt completely at peace. If only life could always be like this, she thought. Sometimes they walked as far as the harbour to watch the boats unload. By the end of the holiday Maggie noticed a change in Ken. He was relaxed, happy and brimming with new ideas and plans. He'd even got a light tan.

"Chap in the pub's given me the name of a man who restores vintage cars," he told her. "Says he's always looking for someone to supply parts. I could make them in the garage."

Maggie smiled in satisfaction.

When they were packing to leave, she couldn't close her case.

"It's all those presents for the grandchildren," Ken said. "You spoil them."

Maggie pulled a face. She thought that's what grandparents did. "There's no room in my hand-luggage either," she said. "I'll have to leave the book. I've finished it anyway."

*

It was evening before Maria and Dolores got around to cleaning the room. The wastepaper basket was crammed with old newspapers, empty water bottles and plastic bags. A book had been left on the dressing table.

"Put it in the rubbish," Dolores said, holding the black bag open.

Maria frowned. "It's a book. You can't put books in the rubbish."

"It's in English. You can hardly speak English let alone read it. What are you going to do with an English book?"

Maria thought for a moment, then her face brightened. "I'll take it my neighbour in hospital. She's English, she'd probably like an English book to read."

As they finished cleaning and making up the room Maria thought about her English neighbour. She hardly knew her, only that she lived in the apartment opposite and kept herself to herself. She hardly ever went out. Maria was going up the stairs the day before when she'd seen the old lady coming down. She heard a crash, a cry, a thump and a groan. Maria called the ambulance and went with the old lady to hospital. A broken collar bone and ankle and some bruising the doctor said. Eleanor had felt dizzy before she fell so they were keeping her in for tests.

"I can't manage the stairs in a wheelchair anyway," Eleanor said.

"Do you have any family?" the doctor asked.

"In England," Eleanor replied. "I don't think we need bother them."

*

Eleanor turned the book over in her hand. A thriller, she thought, how kind of her neighbour to bring it. She couldn't remember the last time she'd read a book – not all the way through. These days she preferred magazines - they required a much shorter attention span. When she did attempt a book she found her mind wandering, or she'd doze off and lose track of the plot.

It had been different when they'd first come to Spain fifteen years ago, her and Tom. She'd had lots of time then, time to read, go walking and sailing. Tom loved the sea. Of course the sea here was quite different from the sea at home: calm azure waters beneath a wide blue sky as opposed to oppressive greyness, wild winds and crashing waves. Tom loved the sea and all its moods and she loved Tom, he was her world. When he died she felt as though she'd been cast adrift on one of those stormy seas.

Laura, their daughter, had wanted her to move back to England and live with her and Paul, but she didn't want to be a burden and anyway she wanted to stay with Tom. He loved this place.

"When I die," he said when his illness took hold, "bury me here among the olive groves."

So they did. They buried him on a hillside overlooking the town where the sun warmed his grave. Eleanor didn't visit the grave, preferring to keep him alive in her mind, although her life changed after he died. There was no more sailing around the coast, discovering secluded coves and bays, no more cocktail hours at the Harbour Club, followed by dinner at a local restaurant, no more socialising with ex-pats. Eleanor couldn't bear the gaiety, the clinking of glasses and the laughter; without Tom it all seemed shallow and pointless.

"Is there anything you need? Anything I can get for you?"

Lost in her memories Eleanor had quite forgotten Maria sitting there. She smiled. "How kind," she said.

*

Maria stood in Eleanor's bedroom holding the list of thing she required. She noticed a suitcase on top of the wardrobe and a small holdall next to the bed. She picked up the holdall and began collecting the things Eleanor requested. A photo in a silver frame stood on the bedside table. Maria picked it up. A man, late sixties, wearing a sailing cap and blazer grinned out at her. His face was tanned and crinkled, dark strands of hair curled around the cap. The pipe clenched between his teeth gave him a rakish air, accentuated by the twinkle in his blue as the Mediterranean eyes. Ah, the husband, Maria thought, and slipped the photo into the holdall. There were more photos in the living room: a wedding group, the bride and groom flanked by Eleanor and her husband, a mother, father and three boys, three boys huddled together, aged between eight and thirteen Maria guessed. The last was inscribed '*To Nan, love Dylan, Henry and Scott.*' Maria frowned. Grandchildren?

She grimaced. She couldn't understand these English people. Why did the old lady live here alone and her grandchildren thousands of miles away?

She remembered her own Grandmamma, a small woman with steel grey hair to match her steel grey eyes, eyes keener than a hawk. She was feared and loved in equal measure. Dressed in black she sat by the back door crocheting, but she missed nothing. A smile spread across Maria's face at the memory. Her parents worked in the fields with her aunts and uncles from early morning while Grandmamma got her and her cousins ready for school. They came home for lunch, eaten amid much chatter and laughter, around a long table on the terrace under the trees.

Grandmamma dished up huge bowls of paella, chicken, chorizo sausages and spiced tortilla. There was fresh baked bread, ham and cheese. Copious amounts of sangria accompanied the meal, orange juice for the children. After a boisterous lunch the grown-ups would settle for siesta while the children cleared the table and washed the dishes before being allowed out to play. Later the workers returned to the fields to make the most of the cool evening air and Maria and her cousins did their homework under Grandmamma's watchful eye. Grandmamma was a firecracker. If they incurred her wrath she'd chase them with the bristle broom and slap their legs. She was strict but they knew they were loved. Maria wiped a tear from her eye.

On the side near Eleanor's chair, an address book lay open next to the telephone. There was only one number on the page, with the name Laura. Maria reached out and lifted the receiver.

*

Several days later Laura stood in her mother's bedroom, folding her clothes and packing them into the suitcase from the top of the wardrobe. She'd been surprised to find her father's clothes still hanging in the closet. They carried his smell, but faded now. How long had it been? Ten years at least. She couldn't understand why her mother stayed. She'd tried many times to persuade her to come home but she never would.

"This is my home," she said.

Laura felt a pang of guilt as she glanced around the room. Of course she'd meant to visit more often but with a husband and three boys it wasn't that easy. They'd have had to stay in a hotel and with the boys at school it would have had to be in the holidays and everyone knew how the costs spiralled in school holidays. Laura sighed. She should have done more. She wouldn't even have known about the fall if it hadn't been for that maid ringing her. She could strangle her mother sometimes – her and her blasted independence.

She folded the last of the cotton frocks into the suitcase. All her mother's clothes were dated and most of them well worn. It didn't look as though she'd bought anything knew since the funeral. Laura sighed.

At least her mother had agreed to come home with her and stay until she was better.

"We'll see how it works out after that," Laura said.

She was looking forward to her mother staying. It would be good to have some female company for a change. Living with four males can be a bit wearing, she thought and the boys would love seeing her, someone else to impress and confuse with their computer games. Dylan was the spitting image of his grandfather, Henry had his quirky sense of humour and Scott had inherited Tom's spirit of adventure. Perhaps if Eleanor saw Tom's legacy and how he lived on in his grandchildren she'd feel less alone.

Laura had been shocked at how frail her mother looked in the hospital. Still, once she got her home she'd be able to take care of her, put the sparkle back in her eyes and the fun back in her life. She thought about her friend Stacey who lived around the corner. Her mother lived a couple of doors away. They popped into each others' houses every day. 'My built in baby-sitter,' Stacey called her mum. Laura envied their closeness. It wouldn't do her and Paul any harm to have a little time to go out together either, she thought.

She sighed, clicked the suitcase shut and carried it through to the living room. She took one last look around the room before going out to the waiting taxi.

In the hospital she collected her mother's holdall and hooked it onto the back of her wheelchair. She picked up the book lying on the side table.

"Hmm. A thriller. Any good?"

Her mother frowned. "Not bad. A bit violent for my taste." She hated to admit she'd been too distracted to finish it.

Laura flicked open the cover. "There's an inscription on the fly-sheet. '*To Daddy love Amy xxx*'. Aw, how sweet." She smiled at her mother and shrugged. "I'll pop it in my bag. It'll give me something to read on the 'plane going home."

First published in People's Friend in 2012

Too Clever by Half

Grandma said it first. "Don't be too clever," she said. "Lads don't like girls who are too clever." That got me thinking. I was bright. I enjoyed school and got a kick out of answering the teachers' questions. I did well in exams and made Mum and Dad proud. They were thrilled at the thought of me going to university. No one in our family had made it past secondary school. I had a pile of prospectuses at home, awaiting my attention.

But I didn't have a boyfriend. All the other girls had boyfriends. I felt like the last book in the library - the one no one wants to take out. I wasn't bad-looking, good skin, clean hair and healthy teeth. I made an effort to look my best and wear fashionable clothes. I read widely so I'd have something interesting to say. I got on well with the girls, but the boys shied away. Tanya, who had a great sense of humour, but little sense about anything else, was never short of dates. Perhaps Grandma was right.

One Saturday, a group of us were sitting in our local coffee bar when the subject of the end of term disco came up. Between sips of skinny lattes everyone was asking, "Who are you going with?" I was the only one who didn't have a date. I tried to shrug it off, as if it didn't matter.

I laughed along with the others, but inside my heart was breaking. I wondered what was wrong with me, but deep down I knew. Grandma was right. I was 'too clever by half.' I imagined a long, loveless life, empty and meaningless. I'd die a lonely spinster with no children

33

and not even a lifetime of happy memories. Misery settled like a lead weight in my stomach.

"You intimidate them," Tanya said, sipping her latte. "You outshine them and make them feel inferior. Boys like to be in charge, or at least think they are." She winked and gave a wicked grin. "Why don't you come to the footie this afternoon?" she said. "Loads of hunky blokes chasing a ball over the Rec. One of them's bound to take your fancy. I'll introduce you if you like."

I sighed. "But I hate sports. I can't tell football from basketball. It'll be a disaster." I swallowed a gulp of coffee to hide my disappointment.

"Do you want a boyfriend or not?" Tanya raised her eyebrows at me. "You won't find one tucked inside the pages of '*The Magic of Maths*', that's for sure."

She was right. With my apology for a social life, going to the footie with Tanya was my best hope of getting a date for the disco. That afternoon I went to my first ever football match.

The wind whipped my hair into a greasy frenzy. I wished I'd worn a thicker coat and wellies. Windburn brightened my cheeks. I couldn't follow the game, so I cheered when Tanya cheered, jeered when she jeered and jumped up and down when she jumped up and down, although she may have just been trying to keep warm. I heaved a shudder of relief when it was all over.

In the club bar afterwards, Tanya introduced me to Jimmy, the team's centre forward. He said he'd been named after Jimmy Greaves, the footballing legend famous for missing out on playing in the 1966 World Cup Final. He was tall, athletic and blonde with swimming pool eyes. His muscles strained to escape the confines of his T-shirt. My heart turned over.

"Great game," I said, beaming my best ever smile in his direction.

"We lost," he said, eyeing me suspiciously.

My heart sank. He smiled at my discomfort and swung into a chair beside me.

"I'm a Gooner," he said. "Who do you support?"

My mind went blank. I crossed my fingers. "Gooners too," I said eventually.

He laughed. "I bet you don't even know what a Gooner is." I had to admit I didn't. "Arsenal Supporter. Arsenal - Gunners – Gooners, get it?" I didn't, but nodded anyway.

"I've met some air-heads in my time," he said, smiling broadly. "But you beat them all. Never heard of Gooners." He shook his head. "Unbelievable," he said.

He offered to buy us drinks. "What are you having?"

I smiled. "Orange juice, thanks."

His eyes widened. "Orange juice? You're kidding?"

Tanya nudged me. "Yeah, she's having you on. Two Bacardi Breezers," she said.

I blanched. We were both under age, but that didn't seem to worry Tanya. We got on quite well after that.

Saturday afternoon footie became a regular fixture in my diary. I thrilled at the envy in the other girls' eyes and the way heads turned as I walked past with Jimmy. He called me his 'little sparrow' saying I reminded him of the birds that flocked around his mother when she put out crumbs for them. When he was with his mates, he called me 'Bird-brain'. I basked in the warmth of his approval.

During the week we'd go to the cinema. Jimmy enjoyed war films and sci-fi. Every Saturday, rain or shine, usually rain, I'd stand on the touchline watching him play. I got used to stamping my feet to stop them freezing to the ground and banging my arms to keep my circulation from stalling. I dreamed of huge scarves that wrap around your head and keep your ears warm. Afterwards we'd go to the club and re-live the match kick by kick. I never did get to grips with the offside rule. A warm glow spread over me when he smiled at my confusion.

He told me about his work as a trainee mechanic. I didn't know anything about engines either, and he enjoyed explaining things to me. Best of all, I had a date for the end of term disco, and one I'd be proud to be seen with.

Tanya was made up about Jimmy and me. "His father owns the garage on the edge of town," she said. "You could do worse."

Meanwhile, the prospectuses sat on my desk, waiting for my decision. When I mentioned it to Jimmy, he said, "What do you want to go to Uni for? It's just like school. I'll speak to my dad, he'll give you a job at the garage. He's always looking for someone to do the paperwork, and you'll be earning good money."

"I don't know," I said. "Mum and Dad…"

"That's settled then," he said and kissed me.

We were going steady by the time the football season neared its end. He'd met my parents a couple of times, but I'd never met his. It was the last home game; the final game was an away match. A week's rain must have fallen that afternoon. It dripped off my coat onto my shoes and trickled in rivers down my back. The pitch turned to mud. I did my usual acrobatics to stave of hypothermia. Then, through the sleet, I saw Jimmy running down the pitch. The ball flew towards him, hit his chest and bounced into the net.

"Goal," I shouted and jumped up and down, relieved that he'd scored. His glare would have frozen sunshine. I withered inside. Tanya pulled at my sleeve.

"It's an own goal," she said. "He's scored for the other side." She shook her head at me. "He'll be in a right bad mood now."

After the game, the air between us crackled. Every time he looked at me, he shook his head. "If you had a brain you'd be dangerous," he said. My insides turned to ice. Tears joined the rain wetting my face. Misery churned like snakes in my stomach.

He downed pints of cider faster than a frog flicking flies. I watched him slowly sinking into a stupor. I pleaded a headache and said I wanted to go home. He followed me to the door. "Still okay for next weekend?" he asked, without enthusiasm. The smell of alcohol turned my already upset stomach.

"Next weekend?" I said. I didn't remember making any arrangements.

He tutted and looked at me as if searching for signs of a brain cell. "Last game of the season. Coach to Brighton. It's an over-nighter. I've booked a room. Don't tell me you've forgotten." The gleam in his eyes left me with no doubt about his expectations.

"I can't," I said. "Not next weekend."

His face fell, his brow furrowed, the storm clouds gathered.

"My gran's coming," I said. It sounded feeble even to me. "It's Granddad's Memorial Service," I tried to explain. "He's been gone five years and Mum and Dad have arranged a special Memorial Service. I have to be there."

His eyes narrowed. First he looked incredulous, then sulky, then livid. He kicked the wall where we were standing. I saw the storm coming but didn't foresee the fury. He swore, then he called me some bad names, then his face turned purple with rage. "Give it a miss," he said. "Your gran'll understand."

"I can't," I said. "I promised and they've gone to lot of trouble."

"I've gone to a lot of trouble too," he said. "It's not as if the old man'll notice is it? He's dead." Then he laughed.

I couldn't have been more shocked if he'd spat on me.

I ran all the way home sobbing. I couldn't speak to anyone, not even Mum. I went straight to my room, stripped off my soaking clothes and ran into the shower. I let the warm water cascade over me, wishing it could wash the dreadful hurt away. I'd really messed up this time. I'd never seen him so angry, and who could blame him? I'd let him down badly. All my hopes for the future drained away with the water gurgling down the plug-hole.

Mum banged on the door. "Are you all right love?"

"I'm not feeling well," I called back. "I think I've caught a cold." I stayed in bed all the next day. Tanya told me he was taking another girl to Brighton. I cried an ocean.

Grandma arrived on Saturday and turned the kitchen into a bakery. "I'm making all your granddad's favourite cakes," she said, dusting flour from her apron. "He had a favourite for every day of the week."

"I remember," I said. "Saturday's was chocolate cake and he always offered to eat mine if I didn't want it." I grinned at the memory.

"That's right. Then he'd sneak into the kitchen and pinch another slice when he thought I wasn't looking." Gran's face softened.

"He said it was for 'Ron'."

"Aye, 'later-Ron'." Tears shone in Grandma's eyes. "Quite a card your granddad," she said. She bustled to the sink and crashed about with the pots and pans for a bit. I left her to it.

The Memorial Service was magical. Mum and Grandma had filled the church with Granddad's favourite spring flowers. Daffodils, lilies, irises and tulips brightened up the walls. I helped set out cups and saucers in the church hall for the get-together after the service.

I'd never seen the church so packed. Everyone remembered Granddad as he'd played the organ for the Sunday services. Today Dad was playing all Granddad's favourite hymns. After the eulogy people came forward to light candles and speak about their special memories of Granddad. Grandma had so many happy memories I thought her candle would burn out before she'd finished. I told them about the times Granddad let me come to listen to him practising the hymns. I'd sit in the front pew, mesmerised, as the music filled the empty church, washing over me like a tidal wave.

Grandma sniffed a lot, said something about hay fever and wiped her eyes with a handkerchief Mum had brought specially. 'I bet Granddad's watching us,' I thought, his eyes would be twinkling with pleasure.

Afterward, I helped serve tea and cake in the church hall. Mum and Dad introduced me to the new vicar and his wife, Reverend and Mrs McGregor. A young lad with dark curly hair, glasses and a worried expression, joined us.

"This is our son Matthew," Reverend McGregor said. "He's down from University for the holidays."

"Matt," the young man said. "Call me Matt." His soft Scottish burr gave me goose bumps. Behind his glasses chocolate-brown eyes surveyed me with an intensity that made me dizzy.

"University!" Mum exclaimed. "How marvelous. Our Ruthie's going next year, perhaps you can help her with the application. She's not sure what subject she's taking yet. Can't make up your mind can you Ruthie?"

All eyes turned to me. My heart raced. I felt a blush creeping up from my neck. I'd had enough of feeling stupid. I took a deep breath. "Mathematics," I said. "I want to study Mathematics."

My mother's eyebrows shot up into her hairline. A slow smile spread, like flames over smoldering coal, across Matt's face.

"Fantastic," he said. "I'm doing Applied Mathematics and Economics. It's a great course, you'll love it." He turned to Mum. "I'd be delighted to help Ruth with the application," he said. The twinkle in his eyes reminded me of Granddad.

First published in Woman's Weekly in 2010

Loyalty

He's wearing a suit: it's his dead father's suit. The trousers bunch tight around his waist, the sleeves cover his hands. He's drowning in the double-breasted jacket, smelling of stale cigarettes, beer and mothballs: an old man's smell.

With his piercings removed and his razored hair sticking out like bog-brush bristles, he feels deflated: a shadow of himself, like an empty, trampled on plastic bottle, carelessly discarded: confidence removed, arrogance quashed, vitality withdrawn. In his street clothes he commanded respect; in his father's suit he feels every ounce of life's rejection.

He gazes around the room at the wood panelled walls, the high ceiling and the glittering chandeliers. He shivers. The judge's bench ahead of him is set high above the well of the court, a plush crimson throne beneath a heavy carved crest. This is his first time in the dock: he's a Crown Court virgin.

The silence is oppressive, like in church where people whisper, afraid of shattering the holiness. Barristers in wigs and robes turn to lean over the benches in soundless communication with solicitors seated behind them. People glide quietly back and forth, gowns billow behind them. The only sound is the rustle of papers and the echoing Tannoy calling cases to court like announcing arrivals at a railway station.

The Judge enters; the Court rises. The Judge sits, everyone sits. TJ confirms his name, Thomas John Watson. The Clerk of the Court reads out the charge – TJ pleads not guilty. He goes over his statement in his head. He'd been at home with Danny all evening. Now it was up to Danny.

Danny's the best. He's looked out for him since their father died. He remembers his father's drunken rages, the thrashings that Danny took trying to protect him. By the time he was fifteen Danny had had more beatings than a front parlour rug. Violence was nothing new to Danny – it was all he knew, the only way to settle disputes or win respect. He stood up to the old man when nobody else could or would. TJ's heart swells at the memory. Danny is hard; nobody disses Danny.

He glances up and sees his mother gazing down, fear and bewilderment on her sorrowful face. She's clutching a crumpled tissue. She's been crying; cries a lot, his mum.

His stomach knots. He pushes anxiety aside, squares his shoulders and puffs out his chest. He even manages a smile for his mum.

At the prosecution barrister's request, the police officer in charge outlines the facts of the case against TJ. He's accused of Assault and Grievous Bodily Harm with Intent on one Mr. Michael Macgregor. One after another the witnesses are called. They all agree: the man they saw attack the victim was wearing a red puffa jacket and distinctive black and gold trainers. No one saw his face. Some say his hair was razored into a zig-zag pattern, others say it was dark, it all happened so quickly…There's no positive ID.

TJ's barrister makes the point that half the young men in the country wear red puffa jackets. It's a fashion statement, not a crime.

The arresting officer is up next, a burly florid-faced man in his early forties. The prosecution barrister holds up a red puffa jacket and black and gold trainers. They're Danny's.

"Can you tell the Court where you found these items of clothing?"

"In the defendant's bedroom, sir."

TJ shakes his head. Can't deny the jacket and trainers were found in his room – no argument.

"Can you tell us why you were searching the defendant's bedroom?"

The constable smiles. "Him and his brother fit the description. They're well known in the area."

The questioning of the forensic officer is more specific. The barrister holds up the jacket and trainers again.

"Have you been able to connect these items to the perpetrator of this vicious attack?"

"Yes sir. We found traces of blood matching the victim on the sleeve of the jacket, although an attempt had been made to remove them. Fragments of glass similar to the glass in the bottle used in the attack were embedded in the soles of the trainers."

"So, you have no doubt these items of clothing were worn by the assailant at the time of the assault?"

"No doubt whatsoever, sir."

TJ recalls Danny coming in after midnight that night. He was still up, playing on his PlayStation when he heard him in the bathroom. Then he came into the room they shared. He looked awful, his dark skin drained and a swelling reddening under his eye. Danny threw his jacket onto the chair with TJ's and shucked off his shoes as he dived onto his bed.

"If anyone asks, I bin here all night – right?"

TJ's only sixteen but he knows the form. Never grass. And he hadn't. All the time on remand, all the questions, interviews, intimidation, never said a word.

He swore an oath the day he joined the crew; he knew the rules. It had been the best day of his life when the crew accepted him, even though he knew it was only because he was Danny's kid brother. Danny watches out for him, and he does his best to watch out for Danny. His feelings overwhelm him. There's nothing he wouldn't do for Danny and Danny'd do anything for him.

"Right," he'd said.

Danny picked one of the red puffa jackets off the chair and pushed his feet into black and gold trainers, the same style jacket and trainers as TJ's. TJ thinks Danny must have picked up the wrong jacket and trainers by mistake. TJ had his head razored into the same zig-zag pattern as Danny favoured and he'd had a ring put into his eyebrow, just like Danny. His mum cried when she saw it: cries a lot his mum.

"See you later Bro," Danny said as he left.

TJ's barrister stands up. She consults the papers in her hand. She smiles as she addresses her questions to the witness.

"The blood on the jacket, can you tell us exactly when it got there?"

The witness looks bewildered, shrugs his shoulders and shakes his head. "Not precisely," he says. "But it was fairly fresh."

"Fairly fresh? One, or two days old, or one or two weeks?"

The witness looks uncomfortable. "There's no way of telling exactly when the blood got on the jacket."

The defence barrister continues. "The victim, Mr Michael Macgregor, is known to the defendant, Mr Thomas John Watson. Isn't that so?"

"Yes, I believe he is."

"They're friends? Quite close friends at one time?"

"I believe so, yes."

"Didn't Mr Macgregor get a tattoo on his arm prior to the attack? A tattoo he showed to Mr Watson? Could Mr Macgregor's blood have got onto the defendant's jacket at that time?"

The witness glances around the room as if looking for an answer in one of the furthest corners. He shrugs. "It's possible I suppose," he says eventually, "although the blood was fresh and no trace of ink."

TJ sighs. That blasted tattoo! Asking for trouble that was. Fancy having Rhianna's name tattooed on his arm. Daft beggar. Everyone knows Rhianna is Danny's girl.

"In fact Mr Macgregor's blood could have got onto my client's jacket at any of the times they spent together. He could have had a nose bleed, or cut himself, and his blood would be on my client's jacket?"

"There was no mention in the report of a nose bleed, or the victim cutting himself."

"But you couldn't rule it out?"

"No, I suppose not."

"And the glass from the bottle. How many of this type of bottle get broken in any one night in the town centre?"

"Well, I don't know…quite a few I guess."

"Couldn't the fragments of glass have been picked up by the defendant's shoes at any time in the week before the incident, or indeed at any time at all?"

"Well, I suppose…"

"Thank you."

The morning drags. Even the dock officers are getting restless, folding their arms, sighing and exchanging bored glances. Soon the nightmare will be over and he'll be able to go home.

Medics and doctors give details of Mr Macgregor's injuries. Sounds bad: worse than he thought. Macgregor's still in hospital; on life support. Danny never said that.

The paramedic who picked Macgregor off the pavement is called. TJ wonders what he can add. The prosecution barrister is grinning from ear to ear.

"Did Mr Macgregor say anything when you picked him up?"

"He muttered something. It sounded like 'Watson', but I can't be sure."

TJ's heart sinks. With the witness statements and forensic evidence it's beginning to look bad. All TJ's got is his brother's word as an alibi.

TJ's barrister moves forward. "You say he mumbled something that sounded like 'Watson'. Might it have been 'What's going on'? It would be a reasonable question given Mr Macgregor's concussed state of mind, would it not?"

The paramedic shrugs. "I'm just saying what I heard."

"But you can't be sure precisely what it was you heard?"

"No…not precisely."

It's afternoon before TJ's barrister stands and opens for the defence. TJ recalls her telling him he doesn't have to prove his innocence, they have to prove his guilt, beyond a reasonable doubt. It's like she said, all circumstantial. He crosses his fingers and hopes.

He's called to the witness box and gives his statement. He was at home with Danny all evening. They played on his PlayStation, drank beer and sent out for jerk chicken.

Then Danny's called.

TJ hardly recognises him in his new suit. He's wearing a shirt and tie and his hair is neatly braided. His piercings have gone and he looks older somehow. He tries to catch Danny's eye but Danny stares straight ahead while he takes the oath.

TJ's barrister stands. "Can you tell us where you were on the evening of 29th April."

TJ closes his eyes.

Danny's voice sounds strange, high-pitched and echoing in the hushed courtroom. "I hung around with some mates until seven, then I went to the cinema with my girlfriend, Rhianna. No I didn't see my brother that night."

The barrister looks confused. "You gave a statement saying you were with your brother. Are you now saying this was not the case?"

"I…I got the days mixed up."

TJ leaps up to shout at Danny. The dock officers spring up and grab his arms, holding him back. His mind spins. He can't believe it. His face pales, his insides melt, the energy slides out of him. He sinks into the chair, disbelief throbbing in his brain.

He shivers in the cool air as the afternoon sun moves across the high windows, sending reflections around the walls. Thoughts teem through his brain. How could Danny do it? The betrayal pierces his soul.

Sickness swirls in his stomach as realisation dawns. If he's acquitted they'll realise they got the wrong brother. They'll pick Danny up – who else? Stands to reason, and in time Macgregor might recover enough to finger him, unless someone else goes down for it first.

Danny's got form. One more conviction and he'd go down for so long he'd need a zimmer frame when he got out. TJ's a first offender; his sentence will be much lighter.

TJ sighs. He glances up at their mother in the public gallery. She's been crying again: cries a lot his mum, still not as much now, not since he topped his father. Stabbed him with a kitchen knife to save his mother from another beating. Danny sorted it. Dumped the body in an alley. 'Drug deal gone wrong,' the police said. Never did catch the killer. Never tried too hard neither.

TJ smiles at the memory, then lowers his head into his hands as the full impact of his situation hits him. He's going down for this. Danny's going to let him take the fall. He owes him and it's payback time. Tears fill his eyes.

He lifts his head, squares his shoulders and sits tall. He looks at Danny, catches his mournful gaze and smiles. It's okay brother, he thinks. I understand. I'll do this for you.

His heart swells with pride. He'd do anything for Danny.

Shortlisted in The Sid Chaplin Short Story Competition and published in Northern Tales in 2011

The Happiness of the Heart

I've tried, Lord knows I've tried. If they gave prizes for trying I'd be right up there on the winner's podium. But life's not like that is it? Life has a habit of kicking you in the teeth just when you think you've got it sussed.

Marc was my first wake up call to life's reality. We met at Uni. He possessed a rare intelligence, wit and enough charm to make roses bloom in December. We were made for each other. He was Romeo to my Juliet, Lancelot to my Guinevere, Mark-Antony to my Cleopatra. We talked, laughed and planned our life's paths together watching the sun set over our urban city sprawl. His path detoured when he met Melanie, a bottle-blonde who battled to get her staple-gun claws into him from the moment they met. He broke my heart into a million pieces.

I took a job teaching English to business men on the Costa Brava. I rented a small apartment overlooking the harbour of the little town. I'd always been drawn to the sea. It was heaven. Then I met Miguel, one of my students. His body, musky and warm, smelt of possibilities and pleasures unknown. My feelings spiralled out of control. I drowned in his ocean blue eyes and curled lashes, swept away by the warmth of his honey-smooth voice and beguiling desire to please. We wined and dined by candlelight and walked on moonlit beaches beneath a vast canopy of stars. His burning kisses stayed with me until morning. He mended my fractured heart. In his passionate embrace I believed his whispered promises.

He left me for what he called 'new challenges'. I felt like a country that had been invaded, conquered and abandoned. My heart was bruised but not broken.

Next came the scuba-diving instructor, Paulo, a sun-bronzed Adonis with bulging biceps and a mega-watt smile. He was so gorgeous I thought he could walk on water, never mind teach me to swim beneath it. We ate oysters fresh from the sea and cooked crayfish over embers on the beach to the sound of the sea lapping the shore. His burning desire and lust rush only lasted as long as I was wearing a rubber suit. Have you any idea how hot it gets in those suits? I left him, heart intact.

In Greece, I met a fisherman who seduced me with knowledge and insight. He quoted Aristotle, Socrates, and Plato sitting under olive trees to the sound of crickets chirping in long grass. We read poetry among ancient ruins beneath a sky drenched with stars. In my heart I knew it couldn't last.

I moved on to Italy. What can I tell you about Italian men? They love their food, their football, their clothes and their mothers, in that order. I taught classes in the morning and had the afternoons free to wander along to the harbour and watch the boats bobbing on the sparkling waves. There's something soothing, timeless and eternal about women mending nets and fishermen unloading their catch, the sea lapping against the boats; a sense of permanence, continuity and agelessness.

I sat on the harbour wall reading and hardly noticed the young man with his easel and paints, until he caught my eye.

"Bellissima," he said. "Please do not move. I have nearly finished."

I frowned.

"Please," he said. "Un momento."

I waited. He pulled the picture from his easel and passed it to me: a sketch of me gazing out to sea as enigmatic as the Mona Lisa. "You are very beautiful," he said. "Please sit for me again."

I sat for him the following afternoon until the golden sun sunk low over the horizon, bathing the sky in its sulphur glow. He was young, innocent and incredibly polite. He took me home to meet his mother, Maria. She welcomed me into her home like a long lost daughter, crushing me in her gigantic arms. We became firm friends.

In the warmth of her kitchen, surrounded by the heavenly aroma of baking, spices and flavoured oils, we drank coffee and talked. She told me about her family. Fierce pride and love shone in her eyes, creasing her crinkled, mahogany-tan face. Her determination was clear when she talked about Gino and her plans for him. "He will be an artist," she said. "He will marry into a fine Italian family and have lots of bambinos." I was no threat.

She was teaching me to make pasta when I told her about Marc and his betrayal. I didn't mention his sapphire blue eyes, his lopsided smile and heart-wrenching grin, his perfect teeth and his habit of chewing his bottom lip when he was concentrating, or running his fingers through his blonde waves when he was perturbed. I didn't even mention how my heart fluttered whenever I saw him, the thrill I got when his lips brushed mine nor the shiver that ran down my spine when his fingers touched my skin. In fact, I hardly mentioned him at all.

"Hmph," she said, slamming a lump of pasta dough on the floured table. "Men, they're like children, always going after the newest shiniest toys when in their hearts it's their favourite old teddy bears they love the best. You have to be blind in the eye." She turned the dough over, and looked up at me. "Bitterness lives in the head," she said. "Happiness lives in the heart when the heart forgives." She banged the dough on the table again and kneaded it savagely with her enormous fists.

I left Italy without sadness. I'm on my way home and not before time. Marc will be at the airport to meet me. He said so in his last e-mail, the two hundredth he's sent since I left. He's asked me to marry him and I've said yes. He's a trier too and Maria was right, the heart overflows with happiness when it forgives.

First published in Woman's Weekly in 2012

The Thirteenth Summer

Unlucky thirteen, Callum thinks as he stomps along the crowded beach. Nothing will ever be the same now his gran's gone. This is the first birthday he can remember when he isn't staying with her. He shivers despite the heat of the day. Of course, his mother hasn't remembered. She never does, unless Gran calls to remind her.

The afternoon heat turns humid. The beach hums with activity, noise and confusion. Holidaymakers fly kites, splash in the sea and play in the sunshine. Their obvious bliss only deepens his mood.

He chooses a spot in the shade of the pier and drops like a sack to the ground, stretching his legs out in front of him. He misses Gran. He imagines her smiling face, creased in all the right places and the laughter in her eyes. He tries to recall the softness of her skin, how she smells of talcum powder and roses, her voice calling him her precious dumpling. He remembers endless summers joyfully spent in her company, the outings, and the parties. How different this summer has been. He picks up a pebble and flings it angrily against one of the wooden pier supports.

The August days drag with stifling heat and misery. He notices a girl standing by the water's edge, gazing out to sea, her quiet demeanour at odds with the noisy confusion around her. He watches her as he mindlessly tosses pebbles at larger stones in front of him. She turns her head and smiles at him, a dazzling smile, bright as the morning sun. The icy misery in his heart begins to melt.

China-blue eyes, framed with the darkest of lashes, regard him and he feels a fluttering in his chest like a bird trying to escape the confines of the cage formed by his ribs. She wears a simple floral frock. Ebony curls tumble around her porcelain face and he is lost in the intensity of her gaze. She reminds him of a picture he's seen in the small art gallery by the harbour. His lips curve into a smile and his heart lifts.

He screws up his courage, tells himself he's nothing to lose, gets up and moves towards her.

He tries to speak but his voice deserts him. His hands tremble. He coughs to clear his throat. "Do you live round here?" he asks, trying to look nonchalant.

"I used to," she replies softly.

"I'm Callum," he says, thrusting his hands deep into the pockets of his shorts in case one should spring out towards her.

"Dorothy," she says. A smile dimples her cheek. "My friends call me Dotty."

"Dotty," he repeats, feeling a tightening in his chest. He's desperate to prolong the moment, wishing it would last forever. "We could go paddling if you like, or go for a swim."

"Oh no, I hate the water, but I love the pier," she says. "Shall we go on the pier?" She spins round and runs lightly up the beach not waiting for an answer. His heart sinks for a moment, then he follows, scrunching his way across the stones, gouging out dents that mark his path as he struggles up the slope.

The pier pulsates with life. Neon lights flash, noisy hurdy-gurdy music from barrel organs competes with disco music from the arcades and the sickly sweet smell of doughnuts and candy floss fills the air. Overhead, seagulls screech and the crashing of the slot machines vies with the call of the showmen inviting them to try their luck on the various amusements.

As they stroll along in the sunshine, Callum tells her about his life with his mother, moving from place to place. "My mother sings in the clubs and pubs through the season," he says. "She comes to a holiday resort every summer. I usually stay with my gran, but she's passed away."

"You looked sad on the beach," she says. "Are you unhappy?"

He recalls his sombre mood of the morning. "Unhappy? No, just a bit lonely. I miss Gran that's all. It's my birthday today and she always made it special." He bites his lower lip to stop it trembling.

They walk on in silence for a while. Dotty is easy to be with, it's as though she reads his mind and understands everything. He notices that she laughs a lot, a gentle, tinkling, irrepressible laugh and when he looks into her eyes he sees the colour of the sky and sunlight dancing on water.

They walk on past the tea rooms. The aroma of fresh baked bread gives way to the salt and vinegar smell of fish and chips. They watch people at the shooting galleries and the various stalls lining the pier. When they reach the end of the pier they stand leaning on the railings. Callum gazes out over the water. A light breeze caresses his face. "It's lovely here," he says. "Peaceful despite the noise."

"It's my special place," Dotty whispers, her eyes misting over. Time stands still.

Suddenly she springs away from him. "Let's go on the merry-go-round," she says brightly. "I love the merry-go-round."

Before he can say anything she's up on the carousel moving between the brightly painted horses, hand over hand along the candy-striped poles with their gold and silver trimmings. As the carousel starts up she sits next to him and together they go round and round to the music, up and down like boats tossed on the waves.

They go round, again and again, then stand and watch the people on the Ferris wheel, the Waltzer, the coconut shies and the rifle range. Children sit spellbound in front of the Punch and Judy Show. Callum can't remember when he's had such a wonderful time. The afternoon flies and people head back to their hotels for their evening meal.

"I have to get back," he says, reluctant to leave.

"I'll walk with you. Where are you staying?"

"A small place up the hill."

They walk together and he wishes he felt brave enough to hold her hand.

On the way, they pass a cycle shop. Callum stops and stares at the Silver Phantom racer in the window.

"Wow, look at that," he says, his face glowing. "I wish I had a bike like that."

He stands transfixed, taking in every detail of the gleaming frame. "One day," he says. "One day I'm going to have a bike like that."

Dotty seems enchanted by his enthusiasm.

Nearing the boarding house he comes quickly back to earth. The euphoria of the afternoon evaporates; his happiness disappears like smoke in the wind.

"Will you be okay?" Dotty asks noticing his change of mood.

"Oh, yes, fine." He dreads his mother being in one of her moods.

The door opens and a cold chill sends his heart plummeting. His mother appears in her dishevelled dressing gown, her straggly hair falling over her face. He smells alcohol on her breath. She ignores Dotty. "Where have you been?" she says. Grabbing him roughly she pulls him into the house, slapping him as she slams the door.

*

The next morning Callum gets out early, while the air is clear and the sky a tranquil grey. He watches two young lads carelessly kick a ball around the deserted beach, envying their easy friendship. All night he has hugged the secret to himself, thinking of nothing but the joy of seeing her again.

All day he walks up and down the beach, scanning the faces of the crowds. He scurries along the pier, around the amusement arcades, the carousel. He can't stop thinking about her. Now and then his spirits soar as he catches a glimpse of her, only to lose sight of her again.

Every morning the freshness of the earth renews his hope as he searches for her. Every afternoon he weaves his way between clusters of holidaymakers on the beach, on the promenade, on the pier. Every evening he returns home defeated. Every night he prays that tomorrow he will find her.

The days melt into weeks and he feels a hollowness around his heart. Desperation alternates with excited anticipation. Dotty, Dotty, where are you? He curses his stupidity for not having found out where she lived or more about her. He must find her, must see her again. Memories of the magical time spent with her haunt him. His loneliness deepens as he retraces their steps, always searching. He fears he has lost her forever.

On the morning of his last day he skulks wearily around the deserted town. It's the end of the season. The remains of summer linger, but soon autumn's chill will bring the cold winds blowing in from the sea.

He ambles along the sea-front, his hands deep in his pockets, his head bowed, his heart heavy. Then he hears a sound that makes his heart race and almost leap out of his chest.

"Hi," Dotty says, dancing gaily around him. "I've got something for you. Come with me."

It feels as though the sun has suddenly risen. Warmth flows through him, love fills his heart.

She runs towards to the pier, he puffs along behind. The pier is empty and eerily silent. A few showmen are setting up, but it's too early for the remaining visitors, still enjoying their breakfasts.

On the pier, Callum sees the Silver Phantom racer leaning against the railings. He can't believe his eyes.

"Where did you get it?" he asks. "How? When? This is amazing."

Dotty jumps up and down in glee. "Ride it," she cries. "Ride like the wind along the pier. Come on." And she's off, running along the wooden boards. Callum sits astride the bike and soon he's riding along beside her.

"Faster, faster," she calls. He rides faster and faster. No matter how fast he goes Dotty's there, running along beside him, her gleaming coal-black hair streaming out behind her.

Faster, faster he rides, the pier seems endless. The wind is in his face, he's never felt so good. He rides on and on.

He doesn't see the end of the pier. As Dotty reaches the railings he hits them and somersaults effortlessly into the air. His feet are caught in the pedals of the bike. Together they somersault over and over until they plunge into the water. Down and down they go, the bike dragging him down further and further. Over and over he tumbles, until strong arms grab him and lift him to the surface.

Everyone agrees, if it hadn't been for the deafening crash when a freak gust of wind blew a stack of deckchairs over, no one would have seen him running along the pier and taking a header over the railings. The noise attracted the attention of a group of divers in a nearby boat and when they saw him fall two of them dived in to rescue him.

A few of the older stallholders recall that a young girl, about the same age, had fallen from the pier at that exact same spot some twenty years before. Dorothy her name was. A pretty girl, pretty as a picture.

Back on the pier, wrapped in a blanket, confusion fills his mind as he waits for his mother. Callum is amazed to see his gran standing with Dotty.

"It's not your time yet," she says. "Go back to your mother. She's had a shock, she'll look after you better now."

He stares. "But Dotty…" he says.

His gran smiles. "Don't worry about Dotty, she was just lonely and thought you were too. I'll take care of her."

She takes Dotty's hand and together they walk back along the pier. Dotty turns to wave at him. She's smiling.

First published in Take A Break in 2014 as The Girl on the Pier

Dinner for Three

"My mother wants to meet you," Rick said and my past life flashed before my eyes.

I looked at my swashbuckling hero, his dark hair curling on the collar of his pristine white shirt, his eyes blue as cornflowers in a summer meadow. "Why?" I asked, seeing my dreams turning into nightmares.

"I just think it's about time you met her," he cajoled, enveloping me in the persuasive warmth of his embrace.

Dinner for two in our favourite Vietnamese restaurant had become the highlight of my week, and Rick my reason for living. I'd never tried Vietnamese food before I met him, but Rick loved it so I learned to love it too. He enjoyed classical music, visiting old houses and foreign holidays so they became my favourite things. Everything he loved I loved. Like bread and jam we were better together than apart.

Six months ago he came into my world like a tornado crossing the desert, picking up everything in its path, swirling it around, then dropping it back to earth. He was a photographer and a free spirit, capturing him was like catching a jewel-bright, tropical bird. I thought I'd won the lottery.

Now he wanted to include his mother.

My ex-boyfriend, John, had a mother. I remember the first time I met her. I was a wide-eyed innocent in love, she welcomed me like a five-year-old welcomes a dose of chicken-pox.

"Mother, this is Claire," John said.

I felt the chill as her gaze rose and fell, yo-yoing over me, like I was fungus growing on a piece of cheese. Not so much a chill, more like a blast from the Arctic. Still, he had chosen me and we were happy and so in love that nothing else mattered. We were closer than two coats of paint on a wall, nothing could come between us, or so I thought.

I hardly noticed it at first, it happened so gradually, like the green slime that creeps across crystal water. "Mother thinks this," and "Mother thinks that." I soon found that Mother had an opinion on everything, an opinion that she was more than willing to share.

I heaved a heavy sigh at the memory. "What's she like, your mother?" I asked Rick as we snuggled up together on the sofa, resolving to reserve judgement until I knew more about her.

"She's wonderful," he said. "You'll love her, and she'll adore you." He kissed my nose.

Wonderful! John thought his mother was wonderful but she frowned on everything I did. She didn't like my clothes, said I wore too much make-up, commented on the shops I used and the food I cooked. She even questioned my choice of washing powder.

I found it unnerving. I began to wonder what she'd think before I could do anything. I couldn't even buy a lipstick without speculating about her opinion.

Fearful of finding myself in a similar situation, I decided to check Rick's mother out. I looked her up on the internet. She appeared in several glossy magazines. In her photos, exquisitely styled grey hair framed an ageless face that radiated serenity. She had an ethereal quality about her. Seeing her picture doubled my gut-wrenching insecurity. An American socialite, she'd married an Italian Count. How could I, a humble copywriter working for a small press magazine, compete with that?

"Let's invite her to dinner," Rick said.

"Why don't we take her to a restaurant?" I suggested.

"Mother eats in restaurants all the time," he said. "A home cooked meal would be a real treat and make her feel welcome."

There was no escape. My heart sank faster than a rock in quick sand. I groaned. "What sort of food does she like?" I asked, determined to make an effort.

"She's lived in Italy, she loves Italian food," he said. "Do one your fabulous pasta dishes, she'll adore it."

My heart sank even further. My fabulous pasta meals were rustled up from ready-made sauces courtesy of our local Italian deli. Easy to please someone like Rick, who'd happily live off Chinese take-a-ways, but a sophisticated woman of the world? That was a different matter.

I worried about it for days, wandering round, looking at recipe books. I took a trip into town to peruse the aisles in Harrods Food Hall and Fortnum & Masons. I thought about contacting one of those expensive catering firms that advertise in the glossies but my budget wouldn't stretch to it. I canvassed my friends for ideas. They just laughed. "It's you she's coming to meet, not Marco Pierre White," they said.

In the library I found an Italian cookery book thicker than an encyclopedia. I might as well have borrowed a book on nuclear physics.

In desperation I went to our local Italian deli to see Rosa. She ran the deli and if anyone could produce a meal to compare to something you'd get in a five star hotel she could. She'd been like a mother to me since I moved into my flat, feeding me up and keeping me cheerful. I knew she'd be able to help out.

"Is Rosa about?" I asked Georgio, her son who stood behind the counter looking every inch the Italian Stallion that he was.

"Mamma Rosa? No, she's in Italy visiting family. But I can help, yes?"

My heart took another tumble. The heavy stone in my stomach rolled over. "Well," I said. "It's a bit difficult you see. Rick's mother is coming to dinner on Saturday and I have to produce a fantastic meal for her. I was hoping Rosa could help." Tears sprang to my eyes. Without Rosa's help I knew the meal would be a disaster. My heart buckled at the thought of Rick's disappointment.

"No problem," Georgio said, his face lighting up as if a bulb had been switched on. "I will cook for you. Leave it to me, piccolina, I will prepare a feast fit for the Queen herself. It will be magnifico." He touched the tips of his fingers to his lips and sent a kiss spiralling into the air.

"I do hope so," I said, but didn't hold out much hope. Doubt nibbled my stomach like a piranha.

By five-thirty on Saturday my tiny flat sparkled. Not one speck of dust remained. I set the table with a white linen cloth, borrowed from Georgio, and my best glasses and cutlery. Pink roses overflowed the crystal vase I'd dug out from the cupboard under the sink, and scented candles wafted yang-yang and jasmine into the air.

Only the kitchen showed any signs of chaos. Haphazardly placed jars of herbs and spices spilled out alongside a liberal sprinkling of flour on the worktop. I propped the heavy library book open at the page for pasta sauce and left it in a prominent position, hoping that the carefully assembled disarray I'd created would convince my guest that I'd spent hours in culinary preparation. Saucepans stood ready for the pasta and pasta sauce.

Then I made a huge bowl of crisp green salad and a tomato and onion salad together with my special recipe dressing. It had a tang of lemon that reminded me of an idyllic holiday spent in sunny Sorrento. I hummed as I worked and even threw a couple of flour bespattered bowls into the sink and left the gouged out lemon peel in plain sight, along with the juice extractor, for good measure.

At six o'clock I was in Bertelli's Delicatessen picking up the meal we would eat that night.

"Antipasto," Georgio said. "Parma ham, salami, pepperoni. Serve at room temperature. Do not put it in the fridge. Si?"

"Si," I repeated, feeling like a first year student talking to the headmaster.

"Tortellini. Into boiling water – three minutes only, add a dash of olive oil. Capisce?"

"Capisce".

"Pasta sauce. Simmer gently, like a lover's caress. Do not boil!" He glared at me as if boiling his sauce would bring an end to all things good in his life.

"No boiling," I said.

"Parmesan – slivers, not grated. Fine curls of cheese and a little black pepper. Nothing else."

I nodded.

"Then tiramisu, the crowning glory. She will fall at your feet when she tastes this. Be prepared."

I giggled. "I'm ready," I said.

"What wine you serving?" He looked at me, his eyebrows knitted into a frown.

I shrugged. "I've got red or white."

He gasped and slapped his forehead. "Chianti," he said handing me several bottles.

"Chianti," I said.

"Fine. Now go. And if this doesn't work out I will come marry you myself."

I laughed. "I may have to hold you to that," I replied backing out of the door with my purchases.

On the drive home doubts began to set in. Who was I trying to kid? His mother ate in the most expensive restaurants in the world and here I was offering her tortellini in a heated up sauce. Not even Rosa's heated up sauce. I didn't know if Georgio could cook, I hadn't asked. He was good looking and had the sort of sex-appeal that should be restricted to small doses, surely it was too much to hope for that he could cook as well. A leaden weight settled in my stomach and tears filled my eyes. My dream of life with Rick was slipping away faster than an eel released into the sea. It was going to be a disaster. I could feel my face burning at the thought of the humiliation I would suffer at the hands of Rick's mother and the hurt in his face when my deception was exposed. There was nothing I could about it so I took a deep breath and ploughed on.

By the time Rick arrived with his mother at seven-thirty I had slipped into the slinky midnight-blue dress I'd bought specially. It had silver trimmings and I hoped that I looked so amazing that no-one would notice the food.

"Mother, this is Claire. Claire, meet my mother Sophia."

"Sophia," I said. I almost curtsied. She was jaw-droppingly gorgeous. Even more glamorous than I had imagined, but I did see a twinkle in her grey-blue eyes.

"Charming," she said. "I'm so delighted to meet you."

I took her soft cashmere wrap and lead her into my cosy living room. It suddenly looked shabby and dull in her presence. Rick poured aperitifs while I disappeared into the kitchen, wishing I could disappear into the wall.

All through dinner butterflies ricocheted around my insides. I could hardly eat anything myself but Sophia was as gracious as she was beautiful. I could see where Rick got his impeccable manners. She complimented me on the antipasto. "Delicious and so refreshing," she said. When she tasted the pasta sauce, she said "Hmm. Oregano, basil and… is that a touch of anchovy paste?"

I didn't have a clue so I nodded, stuffing a bread roll into my mouth, my face as crimson as the Chianti.

"It's lovely," she said. "I can taste the sunshine of Italy melting on my tongue."

After the tiramisu she said, "Rickardo, you should marry this girl, she cooks like an angel."

He smiled. "I intend to," he said. "If she'll have me. You will, won't you Claire, marry me that is?"

Of course I said yes.

After the champagne that Rick produced to celebrate, Sophia helped me clear the dishes.

In the kitchen she said, "You have great taste. Bertelli's Deli make the best pasta sauce outside of Italy. I never could see the sense in cooking when someone else does it so much better." Then she winked at me.

She must have seen the shocked look on my face. She laughed. "I saw the Bertelli bag as I came in," she said. "I never shop anywhere else when I'm in town."

That's when I knew I had made a friend for life.

First published in People's Friend in 2010

Moving On

"I don't know how much longer I can stand it," I said. "I may end up killing her, she's driving me nuts." I was in the local wine bar with Stephi, my best mate hoping for a sympathetic ear.

"I take it you mean Rosemary, your new boss." Stephi eyed me with interest. "I'm sorry Jen. I know you had your heart set on that job. I can see you're upset."

"Upset? I'm thinking of committing murder." I took a swig of Pinot Grigio and grimaced. "Anyway, it didn't have to be me. Anyone from our department would have been better than bringing in an outsider."

She sighed. "Perhaps they wanted new blood, you know, fresh ideas, someone a bit more dynamic than old Mr Bradbury. Everyone knew he spent more time dozing in the office than working. The sales figures have been tanking for some time. She's been brought in to turn things around. I don't envy her that job." Stephi was PA to the top brass and heard all the gossip.

"Well, I'm sure there are other people in the office who could have just as easily done that." I took a gulp of wine.

"Oh I see." A broad grin spread across Stephi's face. "You mean Rob? Rob with the rugby players' shoulders, lead-melting eyes and mega-watt smile? I don't think he's quite what they had in mind."

"Not only him," I said, blushing like a kid caught with her hand in the cookie jar. "But I'd prefer working under him any day."

"Yeah, I bet," Stephi said with a gleam in her eye. She put her glass on the table. "It's always difficult working with a new boss who wants to make her mark and prove to the Board that she's a mover and shaker."

"Well, she's shaken me alright and I'm thinking of moving. Moving out."

Stephi put her hand on my arm. "Don't do anything hasty. I'd be devastated if you left."

I swigged the last of my wine and nodded towards Stephi's almost empty glass. "Do you want a refill? Perhaps I can drown my despair in Pinot Grigio."

The next morning Rosemary called me into her newly decorated office. White walls, pot plants and walnut furniture replaced Mr Bradbury's solid oak and mahogany fittings, his bulging bookcases were gone and beige carpeting covered the floor; the warm mustiness that surrounded him was missing.

Rosemary looked a picture of cool efficiency in a blue suit with her blonde hair piled high on her head. She stood leaning against her desk, surveying me like a teacher surveys an unruly pupil. Rob was there too. He'd pulled her chair around to the side of her desk and sat staring at me with an inane grin on his face. Since she'd arrived they'd had numerous meeting in her office with the door closed. My stomach knotted.

She had a steely glint in her eye as she set out her expectations. "I need you to pull out all the stops, Jen, if I'm to convince the Board that an expansion in this department will uplift the firm's current service delivery performance. This is really important," she said. "I'd even go as far as to say your job depends upon it."

As motivation goes, my motivation went. I'd spent a month getting 'on message', 'pushing the envelope' and 'sharpening my pencils'. Now all I cared about was getting rid of Rosemary.

The next few weeks passed in a flash. Rosemary was seldom in the office. She had back-to-back meetings and was often out all day. Most days Rob went with her and I was left in the office doing the donkey work.

Orders flooded in and I was rushed off my feet. It was so unfair. If only I could think of a way to get rid of Rosemary, perhaps I would be the one going out with Rob.

My opportunity came the day before the Annual Conference. Rosemary called me into her office.

"I'm giving a presentation to Conference tomorrow setting out the additional resources required for direct marketing over the internet. I've set out my plans for synchronicity across functionality but need you to transfer them to power-point. Do you think you can do that for me?"

I nodded. I don't suppose I have a choice, I thought.

"I knew I could rely on you Jen." She flashed me an ingratiating smile. "Can you e-mail it over directly to the Conference Centre ready for the morning? I've got to go over there and check out the arrangements. Thanks."

I met up with Stephi for lunch the next day. "You look a bit chirpier," she said. "What have you been up to?"

"I've got Rosemary sorted," I said, chuckling. "After today she'll probably be moving on."

"Really?"

"Yes. She's got a phobia about spiders you know. There was one in her office when she was in there with Rob. She rushed them both out and got a cleaner to remove it. Apparently even pictures of spiders set her off."

"So?"

"So, when she asked me to type up her presentation about using the World Wide Web as a marketing tool, I thought what better way to demonstrate it than have a spider do the presentation."

"You didn't?"

"Yes. A huge fat, hairy spider moving across every page. Some of them are quite animated." I chuckled. "Well, she did ask me to think outside of the box."

"You idiot!" Stephi glared at me. "It isn't Rosemary who's terrified of spiders, it's Rob. She said it was her to spare his embarrassment. She's not giving the presentation either, she's phoned in sick. Rob's doing it." A look of horror crossed her face. "He'll go mental," she said.

My phone bleeped – a text from Rob. He wants to see me in Rosemary's office – NOW. Oh dear, I thought. It looks as though there's a shortfall in my compliance reality and I might be the one moving on after all.

First published in The Weekly News in 2013

Dolphin Blues

The boat bumps gently against the outcrop of rocks that mark the margin of the bay. I brace my legs and push the lad to his knees in the bow in case he stumbles in the darkness. Not got his sea-legs yet. Not sure if he ever will. A line of boats bob on the tide, an amber glow of lights stretch across the bay entrance, all eyes watching, waiting. Above us the sky is clear and full of stars. I give thanks for the calmness of the inky sea.

I track the dolphin's path by the silver slither of moonlight skidding along his back as he circles in the water. Every time he swerves towards us, the boats close up and swing their spot-lights on the water to catch him in their beams. I see him heading our way.

"Now Davy, now," I shout. I grip my whistle between my teeth, blow with all my breath and slap the water with my paddle. Davy heaves his rattle. A crescendo rises around the bay. Shouts, yells, horns, rattles and whistles break the night silence, rising louder than a home goal roar at St Austell.

My heart is heavy with foreboding. I've seen it all before, man's pointlessness against the power of nature. The dolphin scythes effortlessly through the water, curious but unperturbed.

Boats run together, weaving and turning, churning up the sea. The lifeboat running alongside him is no match for the dolphin's speed and agility. We'd managed to turn the main pod away the previous day, but this one has returned, following an instinct too strong to resist.

We took the boy in after Sam's death. Peggy insisted. Her heart's bigger than an ocean liner. For me the loss was still too raw, too fresh in memory. Three months gone feels like only yesterday. Sam's death hit me worse than a North Sea squall. It's not supposed to happen like that….Forgiveness is an ocean away, the trough I'm in too deep to navigate.

I've been a fisherman all my life, like my father and his father before him, following centuries of tradition. Never known anything else - never wanted to. I worked on the boats when I was Davy's age; so did Sam.

"Sea-water runs through your veins," Sam used to say, but he was different. There was a softness to him I'd never had. Not a weakness though. Sam knew the sea and all its moods and dangers, but he never feared it. He'd work the nets on a pitching deck in a force ten howler, his bright yellow sou'wester the only thing visible in a shroud of mist and fog. What he did is beyond understanding.

Hope of turning the dolphin away is fading. I put my hand on Davy's shoulder. "It's no use lad. We can't turn him. Time to go home."

He gazes up at me, his azure blue eyes wide with dismay. I see his father's face - his wild, sandy hair and his determined jaw. My heart lurches, the knot of pain in my stomach tightens as the years fall away. Sam loved the freedom of the ocean, just as I did. There was no one happier on a good day when the mackerel were running high. I thought he'd stay forever. I never could fathom why he left it all behind.

The dolphin rises out of the water, so close I can almost touch it. "Go back. Go back," Davy yells, waving his arms. The dolphin seems to nod, his eyes bright and what looks like a smile on his face, before he turns and swims away. A huge cheer goes up from the boats. Davy's face glows with joy.

I wait until the dolphin's chatter fades into the distance, then steer the boat back to shore. A crimson dawn spreads across the horizon, gulls screech overhead to greet the morning.

"Why do they do it Granddad?" Davy asks, his small voice almost lost in the chugging of the engine and the sound of the sea. "I mean, why has he come back, when he could be safe in the ocean?"

I sigh. How can I explain dolphin behaviour to a ten year old boy when it's a mystery to me? "It's their nature," I say. "They can't help it. Instinct, loyalty to the other dolphins?" I shrug. "Who can say?" I force a smile and tousle his hair. The dawn light shines on the boy's face, so young, so eager and so like his father. How could Sam have…? I shut my mind to any thought. I bring the boat alongside the jetty. Other boats are tying up and unloading. Onshore the town's beginning to come to life.

We fell out when Sam moved away, taking part of me with him. We never spoke after that. I curse the futility of the wasted years. What wouldn't I give to have him back here? Back where he belongs. Anger rises inside me like a tidal swell, threatening to break out. I bite it back.

Davy helps me tie up at the jetty. "Is it the dolphin we saw yesterday? Is he looking for her?" he says, as if trying to get it straight in his mind.

We'd come across the beached dolphin the day before, its once graceful body inert and glistening grotesquely in the afternoon sun. A crowd had gathered trying to save it but without success. I recall Davy's reaction as he crouched down beside it: the bewilderment in his eyes and his sombre silence as he patted it.

"Aye probably. His mate, like as not," I say.

I've seen nature's cruelty too often for it to move me like Davy, but I saw how deeply it affected him. My heart clenches. My mind spirals back to another time, another dolphin pod, another life. Sam was not much older than Davy when a pod of dolphins beached along the estuary. They all died, gasping for air, stranded along the foreshore of the river. Fishermen are used to loss, but the scale of the tragedy was striking. We did all we could to save to them, but they were hell-bent on self-destruction and there was no way of stopping them. Their deaths hit Sam harder than most. He grieved for them. He didn't speak for a week, locked into deep personal misery. He took flowers to the place where we buried them and sat for hours, gazing out to sea. Daft beggar. My heart lurches as though rocked by a sudden wave.

I help Davy off the boat. "He must have loved her very much," he says, no louder than a whisper. He turns to me for confirmation. I can read his mind, but I have no answer to the question in his eyes.

"The dolphin," Davy says. "He must have loved her very much." He places his hand in mine. It feels small, warm and trusting.

Sam left to work as a roadie for a rock band. What sort of life is that for a man? He married the singer. Peggy went to the wedding. She said she was beautiful. Pale as a lily she was, and just as delicate it turned out. When she got ill, Sam nursed her. Just like Sam to give up everything to be by her side. Day and night by her side, they said. Her death left a broken man and a heartsick boy. But what he did…I could never forgive that. Some call it the coward's way out. Inexcusable. He should have come home. What was he thinking? I blamed myself. Was I too hard on him?

"Perhaps he wanted to be with her forever," Davy says. "Wanted them to be together for always." He takes a breath. "Just like my dad," he says. "He loved my mum very much, didn't he?"

I see the vulnerability in his eyes: like he's trying to make sense of it, trying to find an answer to somehow make it all right. He bites down on his lip to hold back the tears - a small boy trying hard to be a man. A lump rises in my throat. I swallow it. An unexpected surge of feeling for the boy swells inside me, like a wave that knocks you off your feet and drags you, helpless, into the sea.

I can't speak. Locked in silence I nod. I feel ashamed. Imprisoned in my own grief I'd given no thought to his. With difficulty I find my voice. "He loved her more than life," I say eventually. "I guess he couldn't live without her either." My anger ebbs like the tide.

Davy falls into step beside me. I see what Sam did as a betrayal of all I believe in, Davy see it as an act of all consuming love.

Was I wrong? Have I misjudged Sam? I blamed him for uncaring, selfish, weakness. Was it in fact undying devotion? I battle with my feelings. A whirlpool of emotion envelops me. Have I become so hardened I've lost all compassion?

Confusion rages inside me. I search for some sort of understanding. I try to put myself in Sam's place but we're too different. My heart aches for the loss of him.

I breathe in the salt spray that stings my eyes. Forgiveness is still an ocean away but I have a new priority now. Sam's left Davy's future in my hands. It stretches ahead of me like a precious gift. He's given me a second chance: one I won't mess up this time.

We walk up the shingle beach. I feel Davy's small hand in mine and the gap between us closes. I know it won't be easy, there's still an ocean to cross, but the icy resentment begins to melt. I swallow hard. "So, you think you might be a fisherman then?"

Davy's face breaks into a grin. He nods. "The best ever," he says.

"Aye, well, that's as maybe," I say, choking back the tears. "Come on. Nan'll have breakfast ready and she'll skin us alive if we're late."

First published in Debut Magazine in 2011

Recycling Romance

I'm humming along to the radio as I drive up the ramp to the tip but all I can think of is Jake's betrayal. For three years he was my whole life. I thought we'd be together forever, then, six months ago, he walked out and broke my heart. Now at last I'm doing something to get him out of my system forever.

The Civic Amenities Site, more often referred to as the Recycling Centre, has elevated parking bays overlooking a vast dumping area. I back up to the 'General Waste' bay, next to the 'Paper and Cardboard' section.

I turn the engine off and move towards the back of my hatchback, pausing to check on Darcy. She's safely strapped in her seat playing with her favourite pink pig, the one that plays a tune when she pushes its nose. Darcy loves noisy toys.

Satisfied that she's okay, I open the boot and walk to the throwing area. I peer over at the mountain of refuse below. It's huge. At one end a bright yellow bulldozer is pushing household waste into a pile, at the other end a mechanical grabber is scooping it up and dropping it into a metal container ready for removal. A yellow sweeper lorry zips back and forth keeping the path clear. The noise is deafening. It looks like an advert for construction toys, you know the ones where the toys look a lot more exciting than they actually are. It's a different world up here.

I take a deep breath of pungent air and check Darcy again. I put her sippy cup of juice within reach. She giggles as her pig snorts and vibrates in her tiny hands.

I'm ready to start. I clench my jaw in determination. This isn't going to be easy.

The first black bag of Jake's assorted clothes and shoes goes to the Humania Bin. Two more bags contain mementos of our life together: photos, letters, postcards and souvenirs chosen together to remind us of the happy times, love notes he wrote that turned out to be lies.

I hoist the first one into the air and heave it high. I feel a sense of liberation as I watch it sail over the tip and land ignominiously with the other discarded rubbish. I do it again with the second bag throwing it with all my might. As the bag leaves my hand I imagine all the bitter memories it contains going with it. I take a deep breath.

I lift the assortment of electrical items I've brought from the boxes. There's a special place at the site marked 'Electricals'.

A man approaches. He tips his hat, a battered looking flat cap. The stench of the dump clings to his heavy tan overalls. He's a Civic Amenities Site worker, who's so polite I want to rename it the Civil Amenities Site.

"Need a hand?" he asks.

I smile. He takes the broken desk-top computer and carries it to the Electrical section.

The cardboard boxes with dried up roses and other gifts I'd cherished are a doddle. Again I feel exhilarated as I fling them over the wall as far as I can. That's it. He's out of my life forever. There's no turning back.

Darcy begins to grizzle. I realise it's time for her feed and her nap. She probably needs changing as well. I slam the boot shut and open the drivers' door. Where are my car keys?

With a sinking feeling in my stomach, I stare at my empty hands. I had the keys when I opened the boot and began throwing things out. They were gone when I got to the boxes.

I stare again at my hands. There's a jackhammer in my chest.

The man who took the computer wanders over. "Everything all right?" he says.

Dumbly I shake my head. "I've lost my car keys," I manage to say. "They were in my hands before I…" I glance over at the now forbidding mass of rubbish.

He follows my gaze.

His eyes widen in disbelief. He stares at me then walks to the wall to stare over at the tip below.

Darcy wails and throws her pig to the floor. She starts to cry. Big fat tears roll down her soft cheeks. My heart lurches. I unstrap her and lift her out. "It's all right baby," I whisper, trying to sound more confident than I feel.

Powerlessness washes over me. I'm stuck at the dump with a howling child and no way of getting home. My head throbs. The noisy activity of the world around me fades into insignificance. All I can think about are my keys, lying somewhere in that huge pile of garbage.

"Do you have a spare set?" the Civic Amenities guy asks.

I nod. "Indoors, at home," I say.

The silence stretches between us.

"I can run you," he says. "If you like."

I have visions of arriving home in a dustcart. He reads my thoughts. "My car's parked over there." He points to a row of cars below, next to the office.

A flutter of relief flits over me, then my heart sinks further. "My house keys are with my car keys," I mumble. "I can't get in even if I do get home." My frustration turns to anger. How could I have been so stupid?

"Does anyone else have a key?" my would-be saviour asks gently.

I take a breath. "My mother has a key but she lives 300 miles away," I say.

She's not the only one, I think, Jake still has a key but there's no way I'm going to contact him. We stand helpless as the minutes tick away.

"What about a neighbour, friend, anyone?"

"My neighbour's away in Scotland. Two weeks touring. I don't know anyone else here." That's not strictly true either. Jake and his air-head, apology for a Barbie Doll, girlfriend live a few streets away. It might as well be Timbuktu. I wish it was.

Darcy's wailing starts up again. I jig her up and down in my arms to pacify her. I know exactly how she feels. I feel the same.

The bin man takes out his mobile phone. "I can ring a locksmith if you like," he says. "He'll come out in an emergency and if you give me your address he can meet us there."

Pound signs flash through my brain but I've been meaning to change the locks ever since Cheating Ratbag left. I nod.

He makes the call then goes to get his car. I watch over the railings as he removes his cap and steps out of his thick rubber boots. His overalls follow. He throws everything into the back of his nifty looking red Nissan and puts on trainers. He turns to wave and the earth stops spinning on its axis. Without his cap I see a mop of unruly brown curls above a tanned smiling face. In his t-shirt and jeans he looks different - stunningly different. I remind myself that I've sworn off men for life.

He parks his car alongside mine and transfers Darcy's seat. She whines. He produces a packet of biscuits which he hands to me. "I didn't know if…" he nods at Darcy who, seeing the biscuits has turned from a grizzling monster into a giggling flirt. I hand her one. She's immediately placated.

On the way home I notice the smell of the dump has gone completely, replaced by a pleasant citrus tang. I notice his intelligent eyes are hazel flecked with gold and his smile is pure magic.

"I hope you won't get into trouble leaving the job like this," I say.

"No. It's no trouble. I'm Tim by the way."

"Ali," I say.

"Ali," he repeats softly. The way he says it makes my insides flutter and a warm glow flush my cheeks. He glances at me and grins. "I'm not really a bin man," he says. "I work two days a week at the Civic Amenities Site while I'm studying for an MA."

"I never thought you were," I lie. "Anyway, nothing wrong with being on the bins. It's a noble profession."

"It is," he says. "Since I've been working there I've come to have tremendous respect for them. They do a difficult job with humour and commitment. You can't ask for better than that."

We arrive at my flat and half-an-hour and £150 later we're on our way back to pick up my car.

"What about you?" he asks. "I didn't see any sign of anyone else living at the flat. Is it just you and your daughter?"

"She's not my daughter," I say. "She's my niece. I'm looking after her while my sister's in hospital giving birth to Darcy's little brother." I swear his face brightens.

"So you're…"

"Foot loose and fancy free? Yup," I say. Even as I say it I feel a tinge of regret. This is not how I envisaged my life would be.

We arrive back at the site. I want to let him know how grateful I am. "You've been so helpful I guess I owe you a drink or something," I say.

"Something would be good," he says with a speculative gleam in his eye.

I smile. He's been kind and I feel completely at ease with him, but my heart is still bruised. I don't want it broken again.

"I was thinking more of a drink," I say fishing a tenner out of my bag and offering it to him.

He shakes his head. "I'll only take a drink if you come and have one with me," he says.

My stomach knots. I swore I'd never get involved with anyone ever again.

It's just a drink I tell myself and he's not Jake. I write down my phone number and hand it to him. "Give me a ring next week," I say, "when Darcy's back with her mum."

He holds a giggling Darcy while I transfer the car seat. I'm kneeling in the back to strap it in and glance over into the boot. There, in the corner, nestling behind the rear light fitting, are the keys I thought I'd lost. I grin broadly as I realise they've been replaced and, like my bitter memories of the past, I no longer need them.

First published in Take A Break Fiction Feast in 2014 as 'My keys are in that lot'.

A Fool's Errand

"Are you sure you want to do this?" Joyce said, plonking herself down at my kitchen table.

"Sure I'm sure," I replied, her uncertainty greasing my confidence as it gradually slid away. I put the teapot onto its mat, next to the plate of doughnuts.

Joyce stared over the top of her glasses. "Well, if you say so," she said. "But it's bound to be another of your fool's errands and a complete waste of time." She pushed her glasses up to the bridge of her nose and poured the tea.

"What's the worst that can happen?" I asked, as breezily as I could. "We can't find him but we have a good time anyway."

"Or we do find him, get caught and he turns nasty." Joyce grimaced.

"I just want a chance to put things right," I wheedled. "It'll be a doddle, no sweat. Trust me."

Joyce looked dubious, but shrugged. She put her cup on its saucer and picked up the cream doughnut, leaving me the jam one. "All right, if you insist."

So, I booked the holiday in Italy. Butterflies tangoed in my stomach, but the sweet thought of justice brought a deep swell of satisfaction.

When we arrived in Italy the sun shone from a clear blue sky. I breathed in the heady fragrance of jasmine and mimosa. Roses bloomed in my garden of hope.

Our guide, Antonio, was polite and knowledgeable. From his silky dark hair to his polished Italian shoes, he oozed confidence. "Mmm," I said. "I love your aftershave. What's it called? I'd like to buy some for my son."

Antonio chuckled. "It's very expensive," he replied, "but I know a place where you can get it at cost. Don't buy in the market, it'll be fake."

Joyce nudged me. "Hear that," she said. A niggle of discomfort rippled through my body.

On Monday we boarded the coach for a tour of the Amalfi Coast, renowned for its spectacular views. Joyce carried the guide book, pointed out places of interest, and read out their history. We stopped for lunch. I had locally caught fish but Joyce went for the pasta. "You know where you are with spaghetti bolognaise," she said.

We stood on the promenade overlooking the sandy beach and I grinned as I watched a young man disrobe and plunge off the rocks into the rippling waters of an azure sea. I nudged Joyce. She smiled.

"That's where they get the coral," she said, pointing to the base of the cliffs where the water lapped against the rocks. She showed me the page in the guide book.

In Sorrento we found a teashop serving English style afternoon tea, with china cups and saucers. "This is just like home," Joyce said. The café offered a huge variety of cakes. Joyce chose the biggest.

All the while, I thought of our mission. I'd show Joyce that I wasn't the airhead she took me for. Fool's errand indeed.

On Thursday, as we sat sipping our tea, Joyce said, "I don't know about you, but I've enjoyed the trips. Even if we don't manage to do what we planned, I've still had a good time."

"Me too," I agreed.

"It's Naples tomorrow," she said. "Then home."

"I've been looking forward to it all week," I said, with more bravado than I felt. The niggle of discomfort I'd managed to suppress for most of the week surfaced. My insides turned to jelly at the thought of what we planned.

On the way to Naples, Antonio told us how he'd bought a genuine Louis Vutton briefcase from the market for ten euros. "But you must take care," he said. "On our last trip one elderly lady bought a radio in the market, only to find, when she got back to the hotel that she'd been palmed off with a casing with nothing but packing inside."

Everyone sniggered.

When we arrived in Naples we found ourselves swept along with the crowd of sightseers heading towards the market.

"Now remember Antonio's warning," Joyce said. "Watch out for con-men and charlatans. At least half of those Gucci bags are fakes." We both laughed.

We plunged into the market. Merchandise, ranging from silk scarves and knitwear to hand-made shoes, overflowed the stalls. Everything was designer label and all unbelievably cheap. I bought a Chanel scarf and a Gucci notebook. "It's all fake," Joyce said, but I loved it.

Around the square, shopkeepers stood outside their doorways, hands held out to tempt customers in. "Hello ladies, come in for bargains. Radios, cameras, camcorders. Cheapest in Naples." A trader held out his hand, inviting me to shake it in welcome.

I put my hand into his. The strength of his grip overwhelmed me. He pulled me into the shop, trapping me behind his hefty bulk. He let my hand go and picked up a camcorder.

"Best bargain today. Special price for you pretty lady. Seventy euros, you want camcorder? Buy now," he demanded. I began to shake.

"Seventy euros? Really?" My heart pounded. It certainly looked like the genuine article. "Look Joyce," I said. "It's just like the one Tom bought, only he paid at least a hundred pounds. What do you think?"

"I bet it doesn't work," Joyce said, glaring at the shopkeeper. "It's a fake."

"I show you," he said. He spun the recorder around, pointing it at Joyce and me. Then he replayed the footage so we could see it.

"Not the most flattering picture I've ever seen," I said, smoothing down my bird's nest hair.

"Let me try." Joyce grabbed the camcorder and started panning around the room. "Look Caro, it's easy, you try." She handed it to me.

"Let me try it in daylight," I said, stepping out of the door. The shopkeeper rushed to my side.

"You buy now. I pack in box. Guarantee, carry case, everything." His eyes sparkled. "All genuine. No fakes, you buy now?"

"In one of these boxes is it?" Joyce said, turning to point at a pile of boxes by the door.

C-r-a-s-h! As Joyce backed into the shop, she sent a display case crashing to the floor. The shopkeeper dashed back to survey the damage.

"Whoops, sorry, silly me," Joyce said. She helped him gather up the fallen items. "Good job it wasn't anything expensive," she said, edging out of the shop.

The irate shopkeeper followed her. I quickly handed him the camcorder I was holding. "On second thoughts I don't think I'll bother," I said. "Come on Joyce, hurry or we'll miss the coach."

We legged it out of there like two frightened chickens running from a fox. Back on the coach, we flopped into our seats gasping for breath. Joyce said, "Did you do it?"

I grinned and picked the camcorder out of my voluminous bag. "Sure did," I said. "Swapped the empty casing he palmed off on me last year for this beauty. Honour satisfied."

We did a 'high five' and Joyce's smile was so wide I thought her face would fall in half. "So, not such a fool's errand after all," I said.

Oh Mein Papa!

Carrie's hand shook as she read the letter. It wasn't the first she'd had on the subject, but this one was different, it looked official and final. Biting her lip she picked up the phone.

Anger rose in her chest with every breath. She gave her name and explained what she wanted. The receptionist took an age to find someone to take her call.

"I'm sorry," she said. "Mr Wolfe Senior, who's handled your business in the past, is no longer with us. I'll put you through to young Mr Wolfe."

When Carrie told him about the letters he promised to call on her personally to see for himself. Carrie couldn't remember the last time she'd seen her solicitor. Of course it was Mr Wolfe Senior then. It must have been her mother's funeral. He had made all the arrangements. She vaguely remembered a silver-haired gentleman in his late sixties. That was, what, ten years ago?

Carrie made herself a pot of tea and sat reading the letter again. She couldn't believe what it said. The council were ordering her to lop her beloved trees, the trees her father planted a lifetime ago when they first moved into the rambling old house. 'A lasting legacy', he called them: their barricade against a cruel world. Whatever happened on the outside they would be safe on the inside surrounded by tall trees to keep the goodness in and the badness out.

Carrie sighed. Of course her father was long gone; the trees hadn't protected them from that great loss. Still, she couldn't understand how someone else could decide they should be cut down.

Two days later Mr Dennis Wolfe called as promised. Young Mr Wolfe wasn't exactly young, she decided. Mid-fifties at least, about the same age as Carrie in fact. Portly and balding, he wore a navy suit and carried a briefcase. His cheeks were florid but his eyes sparkled clear and blue. She wasn't sure what she'd expected but he looked every inch as she imagined a solicitor would look.

"Dennis Wolfe," he said, and handed her his card. "What a lovely house, in a beautiful setting if I may say so."

"Thank you," she said. "You may."

She showed him into the living room. Situated at the back of the house it overlooked the garden. "Can I get you some tea?"

"That would be lovely." He smiled and the flush on his face deepened.

Carrie bustled around the kitchen making the tea. She'd already set out her best china and a plate of Jammie Dodgers. She couldn't remember the last time she'd had a visitor and she wanted to make a good impression. When she carried the tray into the living room Mr Wolfe was standing near the window by her father's old radiogram, studying his record collection.

"Goodness," he said. "Victor Sylvester, Edmundo Ross, Eddie Calvert, I haven't seen anything like this in years. Do you dance?"

Carrie's head jerked up. "No. No I don't," she said dropping the tray on the table more quickly than she'd intended. That was a lie of course. She did dance but only by herself in the privacy of her living room with an imaginary partner. "They're my father's records. He used to dance with Mother here in this room."

As she spoke, memories crowded her mind: childhood memories of staring in wonder as her parents glided around the room in each others' arms, two people in perfect harmony. "They were so in love," she blurted out, then smiled to cover her embarrassment.

Mr Wolfe appeared far less intimidating once he'd settled on the faded velour sofa with a cup of tea in his hand. The seat sagged beneath him and he leaned forward to compensate. Carrie noticed a small egg stain on his shirt to the left of his Oxford blue and white striped tie. It cheered her considerably.

She showed him the letters. "Can they really do this?" she asked. "Can they really make me cut down my trees?"

Mr Wolfe nodded his head. "Leylandi," he said. "Public enemy number one these days and yours must be…" he shrugged and glanced at the window, "um, at least thirty feet tall? Have you never thought about cutting them yourself? It would give you much more light. There's a whole world outside that window and you can't even see it."

Carrie glared at him. "My father planted those trees," she said. "They're his lasting legacy. I'll never chop them down."

He tapped the letters in his hand. "The council have received complaints, they have no option but to act. They can insist the trees are cut to no more than six feet. That's the most they can do." He sipped his tea and took a Jammie Dodger.

Carrie sighed. She'd had high hopes of Mr Wolfe but these were fading fast.

"So there's nothing we can do?"

"Not a lot."

"Can't we get a preservation order or an injunction? Something of that sort?"

He grimaced. "No one cares about preservation these days, it's all construction, and new builds. This is a Court Order, you have to comply."

"What if I don't?"

Mr Wolfe's eyes widened. He swallowed his biscuit. "As your solicitor I can only advice you to obey," he said. "If you refuse they will prosecute. The results could be disastrous: Contempt of Court, fines, even imprisonment and the trees will still be lopped. It's the law I'm afraid." He picked up another Jammie Dodger. "Please don't worry. I'll get on to the Court and sort it out. I'll try to make it as painless as possible. At least I can arrange for a convenient time…"

Carrie stood and walked to the window. She gazed out at her beloved trees trying to imagine them lopped to six feet. She shuddered. "What about the cost…" She glanced at him. "You know my financial situation."

He pulled a thick file out of his briefcase. "Yes," he said. "I do have some papers. My father dealt with the Trust your father set up. I've been looking into it." The thick file landed with a thump on the table. "There are some things here I don't understand. Perhaps you can help. It's about the Trust…"

"Oh, it's quite simple," Carrie said. "When Father died in eighty two he left everything in trust for my mother and me. I don't know much about it, my father didn't want to worry us and Mother would never talk about it. She went to pieces when Father died. Everything spiralled out of control, so Mr Wolfe Senior, the trustee, dealt with it all. I believe he was a great friend of Father's." She took a sip of tea. "I send him all the bills and he sorts out payments, or rather he did. I'm not sure what happens now. But it'll be all right won't it? If there is a cost the Trust will pay?"

A puzzled frown creased his face. "Do you have the deeds to the house, your father's Last Will and Testament or any paperwork I could look at?"

Carrie shook her head. "No. Mr Wolfe, your father, took care of everything. He must have had them."

Young Mr Wolfe sighed. "I need to check at the office," he said, shuffling the paperwork in front of him. "Please don't worry. I'm sure everything will be fine."

Carrie relaxed. "Would you like more tea?"

"Thank you."

The rest of the afternoon passed pleasantly enough. Mr Wolfe was good company and Carrie hung on to his words. It was so long since she'd had company she was reluctant to let go of this new experience. By the time he left Carrie was sorry to see him go, but he promised to return with details of her father's Trust in a few days time when he'd sorted it out.

The next time Mr Wolfe called Carrie was dismayed to see his serious demeanour. She showed him into the living room and hurried into the kitchen to make the tea. Butterflies jitterbugged in her stomach and her hand trembled as she poured boiling water into the Crown Derby teapot.

When she returned to the lounge, Mr Wolfe was sitting on the settee sorting through his papers, some balanced on his lap and some in a pile on the seat beside him. Frown lines creased his forehead and his usually cheery face looked pinched and grey. The gloom of the day outside descended over the room.

Once he'd arranged his papers to his satisfaction he picked up his tea and sipped it. A reassuring smile flitted across his face, then he began to speak.

"First the trees," he said. "I've been to the council and the Court and persuaded them to take no further action for the time being. I've given an undertaking to hire private contractors to lop the trees. This needs to be done by Christmas."

Carrie nodded. She wasn't happy about it but trusted Mr Wolfe to do best he could for her.

"Good. Now, your financial situation." His face became troubled again. He placed a hand on the pile of papers next to him. "These are papers pertaining to your mother's estate. They are in order. Death certificate, Will, details of the disposal of her estate." He glanced at Carrie. "She left all her personal belonging to you, there are no problems there. It's quite straightforward."

He took a breath.

But, Carrie thought. There's a big BUT coming and he's struggling to get it out. She picked up the plate of cakes and offered them to him. He shook his head. Carrie's heart sank. What could be so terribly wrong that not even her French Fancies could tempt him? "Is there a problem?"she asked.

His sigh was like a balloon deflating; an expulsion of air so huge it flooded the room with foreboding. Another blow the trees can't protect me from, Carrie thought. She waited for him to gather himself enough to speak.

"It's your father's papers," he said. "Important documentation is missing. I can't understand it. My father was always so meticulous and yet…" He flicked through the papers on his lap. "Letters, bills, receipts - the paper trail of a man's life and yet…" He shrugged. "Nothing of any substance. I wondered whether you might perhaps have something, anything…Death certificate, details of his funeral?" Bewilderment clouded his eyes.

"Is that all? That's easily explained," she said, relieved that it was only missing paperwork. Not surprising really, after all it had been nearly thirty years.

"It was during the Falkland's War, chaos everywhere. My father served in the Navy. His ship went down and he was lost at sea." She put her cup and saucer on the table and picked up an elaborate silver-framed photo of a man in naval uniform and passed it to Mr Wolfe.

He stared at it. "A handsome man," he said and handed it back to her.

"My mother thought so." Carrie set the frame back on the sideboard. "She was so proud." She picked up her tea and sipped it. "I was away, nursing in Nuneaton when he died. Mother was devastated. She never recovered her health. I came home to nurse her." Carrie paused, lost in memory. "Such rages she had…mood swings like you'd never believe. One minute dancing on clouds, the next so far down only the devil could reach her." Carrie's eyes shone with unshed tears. "One day I found her in here, in this very room. She smashed that picture and all the others. I had to call the doctor to sedate her. Other days she'd lie in her bed lost in grief." She shook her head. "So sad," she said and reached out to pick up another photo, similarly framed.

"This is Mother." She passed him the picture of a striking woman exuding an air of ethereal tranquillity.

"Extraordinary," he said. "She's quite lovely."

He smiled at Carrie. "You've inherited the best of both of them," he said.

Carrie's heartbeat changed from a slow waltz to a frenzied samba.

"Can I get you some more tea?" she said.

While they drank Mr Wolfe showed Carrie the papers relating to her father's estate. He was still concerned about the missing documentation. "It should be here," he said. "Even in the case of the death of a serving officer, there should be paperwork. Are you sure you have nothing?"

Carrie confirmed she had no papers at all, she'd simply relied on Mr Wolfe Senior to deal with everything. "Is it important? Surely everyone loses stuff over time." She offered the French Fancies again.

"I suppose I can get copies," he said, taking a pink one. "The Ministry of Defence, Somerset House, the Probate Office, the papers must have been registered somewhere. Leave it to me. I'll sort it out."

Carrie felt sure he would.

When he had gone Carrie put her father's favourite record on the radiogram. The haunting notes of Eddie Calvert's golden trumpet playing *Oh Mien Papa* filled the room. Carrie closed her eyes and spun around in the arms of her new imaginary partner. When the music stopped her heart kept on dancing.

On the day of his third visit, November mist swirled in the air, shrouding the trees. Carrie lit a fire in the lounge, did what she could to tame her auburn hair and put on her best frock. She left a couple of more recently purchased albums on the radiogram, hoping he might notice. She hadn't enquired about his taste in music but knew in her heart it would be the same as hers.

Mr Wolfe made his way through to the lounge and Carrie went to the kitchen where the tea tray was already prepared. When she carried it in she was surprised to see him on the settee with his briefcase open at his feet, but with no papers taken out.

She set the tray on the table, poured, passed him his tea and waited.

He raised the cup to his lips and sipped. "I've arranged for contractors to call next Thursday to lop the trees. I hope that's not inconvenient," he said.

Carrie glanced towards the window and sighed. "*Que Sera Sera*," she said.

"Good. Now your father's estate…" He took another sip of tea. "The thing is…" He swallowed. "The thing is…" He dipped his hand into his briefcase and pulled out a batch of papers. "The thing is…" His eyes scanned the papers as though looking for an escape. He glanced up at her. "You've never married have you?"

"Married? Me? No never." A terrible fear gripped her. "Are you married Mr Wolfe?" she whispered as dread squeezed her throat.

"Who me?" he said, taken aback. "I'm divorced. Eight years now. Two surly teenage drains on my resources but I hardly ever see them."

Carrie's heart, which had suspended its beat, pattered faster than a tap dancer's double tap. "Oh," she said and offered him a Viennese Whirl.

He shook his head. "There's no easy way to say this," he said, "but your father wasn't lost at sea in 1982. He divorced your mother that year and the following year he married a young lady named…" he checked his papers, "Heather Barrington. Six months later they had a daughter – Tanya. Your father died of lung cancer in 1998."

The blood drained from Carrie's face. His words flew around her head like a thousand angry bees. She struggled to absorb what he was saying. Heather Barrington? Heather Barrington! She'd gone to school with Heather Barrington.

"Your mother must have known. She should have said…"

Carrie's jaw clenched. The room began to sway.

Mr Wolfe took a half bottle of brandy out of his briefcase, leapt to her side and held a capful to her lips. She sipped and then gulped. He poured another capful into her cup, topped it up with tea, added a splash of milk and handed it to her.

"This'll make you feel better."

Carrie tried to drink but bile rose from her stomach. "Excuse me," she said. She stood as elegantly as she could and tottered to the kitchen. She splashed her face and gripped the side of the sink until the nausea abated. Gracious, she thought, what will Mr Wolfe think of me? She patted her face with a towel and turned to see him standing in the doorway, looking deeply concerned.

She flapped her hands and bustled past him back to her seat in the lounge.

"I'm sorry," he said.

"Please," she said, waving her hand. "I'm fine – just a little shocked."

He sank onto the settee opposite her. "The thing is…" he said.

Oh God she thought.

"The other thing is…his Will and your trust fund." He took a breath. "According to the terms of the Will and the Deed of Trust, this house is yours to live in for your lifetime. In the event of your marriage the house and your trust fund become yours as a gift. However, if you die unwed and without issue the property is to be sold and the proceeds, together with the residue of your trust, a substantial amount I might add, go to his sole beneficiary Tanya, your half-sister."

Thoughts raced like wild hares through Carrie's brain. She took a breath, rose, walked to the window and stared out. The clock on the mantelpiece ticked the minutes away.

She stared at the trees and felt a deep sense of betrayal. Time stretched longer than War and Peace. She felt numb, dumbstruck.

Eventually she spoke. "Next Thursday," she said, "when the contractors come, have them remove the trees completely. Raze them to the ground."

She moved away from the window, tipped both the silver-framed photos face down and went to the radiogram. She picked out an Abba album selected the track *The Winner Takes it All* and set it to play.

"Now, tell me Mr Wolfe," she said. "Do you dance?"

First published in Scribble Magazine in 2012

The Magician

They suspected Daniel Dynamic because he was a Magician. He could pull a rabbit out of a hat or make a woman disappear. It was this last trick that caused all the trouble. If it hadn't been for Alain Du Beck, the female impersonator, he'd have got away with his shenanigans.

It was the week of the Bournemouth Festival. The Lower Gardens had been transformed into a Victorian pleasure garden. It was to be a week of glorious spectacle including classical concerts, music hall entertainments, dining, dancing, fireworks and even a hot air balloon.

Daniel and Louisa booked into the nineteenth century Bella Vista Hotel. The hotel boasted a genuine Victorian fireplace in the lounge. Another attraction was the promise of an exhibition showcasing a collection of Victorian jewellery, including a replica of the sapphire and diamond brooch given by Prince Albert to the Queen which she wore on her wedding day. That was certain to be worth a look.

It had been a long drive and Daniel left Louisa to freshen up in their room while he went to the theatre to check the arrangements. He'd hoped to unload the van and leave his props there, but to his horror found there'd been a mix up and they couldn't take anything in until the next morning. He didn't want to leave his stuff in the van overnight as the locks were a bit dodgy, so to his dismay, his precious props would have to be stored at the hotel.

"You can leave them in my office," the hotel manager said and gave Daniel a key.

Daniel sighed with relief. "You've saved my life," he said. The thought of lumping his stuff up the stairs to their room on the third floor had made his heart sink. An elderly porter and the young man on reception helped with the unloading and storing in the office.

Afterwards, on his way up to his room Daniel ran into Alain Du Beck. They'd both been in the business for longer than Daniel cared to remember and Alain and his wife were like family.

"Daniel," Alain said. "I didn't know you were staying here. Is your charming wife with you? You must both join me for dinner."

Daniel blanched. His wife had never in her life been charming but it was an invitation he could hardly refuse from someone he'd shared a stage with on so many occasions. Daniel and Alain ate in the hotel restaurant. Daniel gave his wife's apologies. "She's a bit under the weather," he said. "So I'm afraid you'll just have to put up with me." Alain's wife never travelled with him.

The evening passed pleasantly enough as they talked about the Festival where they would performing. Daniel had a steak tender as a lover's heart and Alain had the salmon. Daniel had a sandwich sent up to Louisa in their room.

The next morning dawned bright and sunny. At breakfast Alain remarked again upon Daniel's wife's absence.

"She's still unwell," he said.

"Perhaps you should call a doctor?" Alain suggested.

"No, I'm sure she'll be fine later on. A touch of summer flu, nothing serious," he lied, without even blushing.

After breakfast Daniel and Alain went into the lounge for coffee. The curator of the exhibition was there and a couple of ladies also enjoying their morning pot of tea. The jewellery had yet to be put on display.

Feeling sociable Daniel decided to entertain his fellow guests with some magic tricks. He turned to the curator of the forthcoming exhibition, took his hand in greeting and surreptitiously slid his gold watch from his wrist. The curator looked properly chastened when Daniel produced his watch, wrapped it in a hanky and smashed it to smithereens against the Victorian fireplace. Then he persuaded one of the ladies to give him her antique aquamarine dress ring.

"You're not going to smash that up too are you," she said, laughing nervously.

"No. It's too beautiful for that," he joked. He wrapped it in a hanky and made it disappear.

They were both suitably impressed when the ring appeared in the curator's jacket pocket and the intact watch was found in the young lady's handbag. Daniel thrilled at the ease with which he had fooled them.

"Must be a heavy responsibility," the young lady said to the curator. "I mean, security and that. So easy to lose one's jewellery isn't it?" she said wistfully.

The curator smiled. "No problem," he said. "All locked away in the manager's safe. I put it there myself." He oozed reassurance. Daniel thought he looked a bit shifty.

After coffee, ably assisted by the staff, Daniel carried his gear out to the waiting van.

He was just about to get into the van for the drive to the theatre when the hotel manager came running out.

"There's been a theft," he said. His face burned so bright you could have toasted crumpets on it. "I've called the police. Nobody leaves. Everyone will be searched."

He ushered all the guests, including Daniel, into the lounge.

"It's the Queen's Sapphire – it's gone," he said. "When the curator opened the safe this morning the brooch had gone - vanished into thin air." He glared at Daniel. Daniel knew exactly what he was thinking.

The police interviewed all the guests and searched the hotel from top to bottom. They even searched Daniel's van. They found nothing, except that Daniel's wife was missing.

"I haven't seen her since she booked in," the receptionist said.

Alain said he hadn't seen her at all – in fact no one had seen her since she arrived. A police constable checked Daniel's room. There was no sign of Louisa anywhere. All her things had gone. She'd disappeared, just like the Queen's brooch. Apart from the curator Daniel was the only one who'd been in the manager's office that morning.

All eyes swivelled to stare at Daniel. He felt the red hot daggers of suspicion headed his way. What could he say? He couldn't tell them the truth about luscious Louisa, how she'd left in a huff when he told her she'd have to stay in the room as he couldn't afford for Alain to see her. Alain would tell Daniel's wife Edna about Louisa and all hell would break loose.

"You liar," she'd screamed at him. "You promised me a week of fun and frolics. You said we could spend time together. You said you loved me. You never said I'd be holed up like some fugitive or someone you was ashamed to be seen with." Tears streamed down her face twisted in rage. She'd thrown the lamp at him, the kettle, the teacups, the cushions. He'd beat a hasty retreat and when he returned after dinner she was gone. He had hoped that when she'd calmed down she'd see reason…

He couldn't even tell them his wife was safe at home in case they rang her. Cold sweat ran down his back. If Edna found out about Louisa her retribution would be brutal, life threatening even, no, he couldn't risk that.

"She's probably gone for a walk," he said, heart pounding.

"What with her suitcase? Her clothes are gone - so's the missing brooch." The police inspector eyed him sceptically. "I think you'd better come with me."

Daniel glanced around helplessly, looking for some support. None was forthcoming.

He knew it was Louisa. She'd set him up. Stupidly he'd left the keys to the manager's office in his room when he went out to dinner. This was Louisa's revenge ... she'd learned a thing or two on the circuit. The safe in the manager's office would be a doddle to an expert like Louisa. Her father was a safe-cracker. Daniel's heart turned over, his mind raced. If only he could get out of this cell, he could find her and prove it. All he needed was a way out – shouldn't be too difficult, he thought, after all he was the master of misdirection, the illustrious illusionist, the Magician.

First published in The Weekly News in 2014

Hot Chocolate and Yellow Oilskins

Rain battered the windscreen as Julie drove along the country lane. The journey to her rented cottage in Cornwall had taken longer than she'd expected; she'd hoped to arrive before dark. She hated the dark. She peered into the gloom. On either side of the road hedgerows rose steeply, making it appear even murkier. Thunder rolled across the deepening October sky. She wasn't used to driving in the country. In town the streets were always bright with light.

A flash of headlights sweeping fast around the bend momentarily blinded her. The driver sounded his horn. Dazed, Julie slammed on the brakes and instinctively jerked the steering wheel to the left. The van skidded on the mud spattered road and slid into the ditch. A black Land Rover, its lights blazing, flashed past, its horn blaring. Shaking with shock, Julie watched its red tail lights recede into the distance.

She took a breath to calm her thudding heart. Nothing was going right for her today. If she hadn't taken a wrong turning and got lost she'd have been here in daylight. Now she was in a ditch, probably miles from anywhere and completely alone. Battling frustration she was beginning to regret her decision to move to Cornwall. In London she'd had a nice flat, a car and her own budding business. What had possessed her to throw it all up, load all her possessions into a van and drive to a cottage she'd never even seen, having picked it off the internet?

It was Rich of course; Rich, the bonkers banker who'd broken her heart. She felt a tightening in her chest as his face flashed into her mind. Biting back the tears she put the van into reverse and attempted to back-out of the ditch onto the road. The wheels spun. A fresh wave of despair hit her; a ball of anger formed in her stomach. The driver of the Land Rover had practically forced her off the road. He must have seen her and he didn't even slow down. He's probably laughing his head off by now, she thought. She banged her hands helplessly on the wheel.

Several more attempts to get out of the ditch proved futile. Shivering in the wet she climbed out of the van; her feet sank in the mud. Her small purple van, freshly painted with the name '*Julie's Jewels*', was firmly stuck.

Fighting off the desolation that threatened to engulf her, she searched in her bag for her mobile phone. The display showed 'no signal'. "Arrrrrggggh," she screamed and threw the phone into the van. She wasn't even sure how far it was to the cottage. She was just about to trudge along the lane in the direction she had been travelling when a tractor, its lights dancing in the sleeting rain, bounced towards her.

The tractor stopped. The driver, wearing heavy oilskins, jumped down. Hands on hips, shaking his head he stared. "You'm be proper stuck," he said.

Relief, gratitude and hope flooded over Julie but the anger lingered. "Some maniac in a black Land Rover forced me off the road."

A flash of lightening lit up the farmer's florid face. "Aye, that'll be Adam Trevelyan," he said. "Where you'm be heading?"

"Trebarra Cottage. I've rented it for six months."

"It's half-a-mile on." He chuckled. "Adam'll be your neighbour."

Julie's face flushed hotter than a bonfire on firework night. Great, she thought.

The farmer attached a rope to Julie's van and pulled it clear of the ditch. He got back onto his tractor. "Good luck," he called as he drove away.

Still seething Julie got back into her van and drove to the cottage. So, she thought, that idiot driver is my neighbour. Well, she wasn't feeling particularly neighbourly.

A wood-burning stove in the kitchen and open fires laid in all the rooms gave the cottage a cosy feel. With its low ceilings, colourful rugs and numerous pots of dried flowers it felt homely despite the cold outside. The dresser in the parlour held an oil-lamp which Julie guessed was for emergencies. She smiled when she saw the electric kettle and microwave in the kitchen. Hot chocolate and a hot-water bottle soon restored her temper. By the time her friend Felicity arrived for a visit a few days later, Julie had made herself quite at home.

"I've brought supplies," Felicity said handing her a box containing half-a-dozen bottles of wine. "Good job too. I didn't realise you'd be so isolated. I got lost but thankfully your neighbour put me right." She sighed. "Now I can see why you've been so quiet. Keeping him to yourself eh? Not that I blame you. He's gorgeous."

"Gorgeous? He's a maniac." Julie told her about her mishap on the road. "If you must know I've never even spoken to him."

She'd seen him coming and going in his Land Rover but, in view of his cavalier behaviour on the road, she didn't think she should be the one to extend the hand of friendship. "I've been busy working on a commission. Want to see it?"

It was the commission from a large chain of exclusive stores that had enabled Julie to rent the cottage in the first place and to follow her dream of having her own jewellery store in the fishing village where she'd spent so many happy childhood holidays. She couldn't wait to show Felicity her latest designs.

"What do you think?"

Felicity gasped. She fingered the tiny ceramic beads. "They look like miniature chocolates," she said. "How clever."

"I'm calling it my Hot Chocolate Collection," Julie said proudly.

Felicity picked up a couple more. "This must be an orange cream and this one a caramel. So sweet." She glanced at Julie. "This one's definitely you – a strawberry delight, all soft and gooey in the centre."

Julie laughed. "And this is you," she said picking one up. "A hazelnut."

By the time they'd had dinner and a bottle of wine by a roaring fire they had assigned chocolates to all their friends. "What about Mr Tall-dark-and-handsome next door?" Felicity asked sipping her wine. "He must be a mega-bar of lush champagne truffle at least."

Julie shook her head. "He's a plain chocolate brazil – smooth and tempting on the outside but teeth-breakingly hard inside."

Felicity raised her eyebrows. "So you do like him then," she said, with a mischievous glint in her eye.

Julie laughed. She hadn't missed her neighbours' obvious appeal but she was still reeling from her break-up with Rich and wasn't looking to get involved with anyone new anytime soon.

The next morning they went to the harbour where Julie was hoping to sell some of her jewellery to the local shops along the quay. The sun had broken through the clouds and promised a bright day. Gulls screeched in an opalescent sky and boats bobbed on tranquil waters. Julie's heart softened, filled with a kaleidoscope of childhood memories. She recalled the colourful stone buildings around the harbour, the cramped, narrow streets, cosy pubs and idyllic days spent exploring rocky coves or playing on sandy beaches.

"Oh look," Felicity said. "There's an open day at the lifeboat station. We must go and support them. They're all volunteers and real heroes. Come on."

Julie followed her along the quay to the lifeboat station. The farmer who'd rescued Julie was manning one of the stalls. "Hello there," he said. "Settled in all right are you?"

"Thanks to you," Julie said. "Lucky you happened along."

The farmer chuckled. "Weren't luck," he said. "Nay, it were Adam there." He nodded in the direction of a man in yellow oilskins Julie recognised at her neighbour, the owner of the Land Rover. "Rang me soon as he got to the main road. He were on a shout see – couldn't stop hisself and there's no signal in lanes."

Julie coloured. "On a shout?"

"Aye. Coxswain of the lifeboat. Nasty night to go out but when there's a boat in trouble…"

Julie's heart turned over. So that's why he was racing along the lane. She'd got him all wrong. She'd seen him as some crazy tearaway, when in fact he was the complete opposite and far from ignoring her plight as she'd thought, he'd been responsible for her rescue. She felt stupid for jumping to such unwarranted conclusions about him.

Felicity nudged her. "We must go and thank him – mustn't we Julie?" She grabbed Julie's arm and dragged her over to where the coxswain was securing the boat.

"I hear you saved the day when Julie got stuck in a ditch," Felicity said.

He looked up, his gaze unashamedly focussed on Julie. Interest shone in his melting chocolate eyes. "Always happy to help a lady in distress." He held out his hand. A broad smile spread across his face. "Adam," he said.

Reluctantly Julie took his hand and caught her breath. The warmth of his touch travelled up her arm straight to her heart. He's not a brazil nut, she thought, more like a cherry liqueur, luscious, rich, bittersweet and surprising.

"Glad to see you're okay. Them lanes can be treacherous if you'm not used to 'em," he said.

Julie's heart pounded. She'd harboured such bad thoughts about him and here he was being so friendly. She felt doubly dreadful.

"Please to meet you," she stuttered. She had the strangest feeling bubbling up inside her, like frothy hot chocolate. She noticed the sea-spray in his black as the night hair and wondered if his lips tasted of salt, then chided herself for her foolishness. Embarrassed she pulled her hand away. "Well, thanks anyway," she said blushing furiously.

"I'm sure he's used to that," Felicity said as they walked back to the harbour.

"What?"

"That reaction he gets when meeting young unattached females."

"What reaction?"

"You know the one - the way you melted like butter on hot crumpets when he shook your hand."

"I did not."

"Yes, you did."

"Did not." Julie huffed and stomped towards a souvenir shop.

"Did," Felicity called after her. "I saw you."

At the end of the week Julie waved Felicity goodbye. Her holiday had flown. She sighed. The nights were drawing in, the sky already darkening. It was the first time she'd ever felt so isolated. She flicked on the light switch – nothing happened.

She went into the parlour and tried that light – again nothing. There was no light in the kitchen or power to the kettle. She glanced out of the window, across the field she saw lights dotted like gemstones on the horizon.

Her first thought was that it must be a power cut, hence the oil lamp in the parlour. She tried to light the lamp but acrid black smoke filled the room. The darkness was deepening. Julie shuddered. "This is stupid," she said out loud as the irrational childhood fear rose up inside her. "Stupid, stupid, stupid," she berated herself, tears stinging her eyes. Through the window she saw lights twinkling in Adam's cottage.

Must be a fuse, she thought. She went out to the van to retrieve her torch. Eventually she found the fuse box under the stairs. All the fuses were intact.

She glanced again at Adam's cottage, the windows ablaze with light. There was nothing for it but to go and ask if he could help.

She squared her shoulders, fixed a smile on her face and knocked on the door. The door opened; the chink of light spreading until she was bathed in it. She drew a breath. Even without his oilskins his powerful build was obvious. "I don't seem to have any light," she said. "No electric at all. I wondered if you could help, your cottage doesn't appear to be affected."

"Power's down. You need to fire up the jenny," he said.

"The jenny?"

"In the shed."

"The shed?"

"I'll come over," he said. "Shouldn't take a minute."

She followed him to the outbuilding behind the cottage. She'd thought it some sort of garage but now saw it housed a fair sized generator. She held the torch while Adam checked for petrol and started the motor. Julie watched mesmerised as he worked. His movements were economical, his quiet efficiency impressive. As soon as the engine fired the lights in the cottage sprung on.

A weight lifted off Julie's shoulders. "Looks like you've rescued me again," she said.

"My pleasure." He took a step towards her. Her heart raced, her mind whirled.

"I've got some pierce and ping in the freezer if you're interested," she said. "It's the least I can offer after you've saved me again."

He smiled. "Pierce and ping – sounds wonderful."

Julie warmed to him as they sat together on the marshmallow-like sofa in front of a blazing fire, drinking wine. She felt sure he was an excellent cook and his enjoyment of the pierce and ping merely politeness. He explained to Julie how to fire the jenny and keep it topped up ready for emergencies.

He talked about his work on the boats and his pride in gaining the position of coxswain of the lifeboat. She told him about her jewellery designs and her ambition to open a jewellery store in the area. "Don't suppose you know of any suitable premises going spare?" she said.

His face clouded over. His eyes narrowed. He shook his head. "I should be going," he said. "Early tide tomorrow." His abrupt departure left Julie astounded. She felt a tug at her heartstrings and surprisingly bereft as she stood in the cottage doorway watching him walk away.

She reminded herself of her decision to come to Cornwall to make a fresh start and follow her dream and that didn't include any romantic involvements thank you very much. Adam had cooled off when she'd mentioned her plans to stay. Perhaps it was better to keep it that way; still she couldn't deny the stab of disappointment pricking her chest.

Over the next weeks and up to Christmas Julie pursued outlets for her jewellery all along the coast. Wherever there were souvenir or gift shops she approached them with samples of her Cornish Craft Jewellery lines. She made several trips to London and gained a further commission to design a collection she called Blatantly Beautiful Bling using sparkling crystals. For the Christmas market she put together jewellery making kits which proved to be very popular.

She wasn't particularly watching out for Adam's comings and goings, but couldn't help being aware of his presence. She became glad to see the lights in his cottage when she returned in the dark; her heart lifted and her feeling of isolation lessened. His greetings were always friendly. When she asked his advice he showed her how to light the wood-burning stove in the kitchen and taught her the ins and outs of keeping a dry wood-pile. There was kindness in his eyes and warmth in his voice. Nothing was too much trouble. Perhaps she had misjudged him again. Or was he being friendly only because he didn't think she was staying?

Despite what she saw as Adam's disapproval, with a secure income she felt able to look for shop premises. She tried all the outlying villages but her search was fruitless. Every place she looked at was either too big, too expensive or had no passing trade. She was beginning to despair of ever find anywhere suitable until one day, walking along the quay, she noticed an empty half-shop at the end of the parade, situated immediately before the steps leading up to the cliff path that meandered around the headland and onto the next town.

She went into the café next door, ordered a hot chocolate and plate of fish and chips and asked the proprietor about the vacant premises.

"Bless my soul me dear, bin empty for years," the lady told her. "Far as I know it's never been for rent. I never seen any boards or nuthin any road."

Julie watched the passing trade; walkers bundled up against the cold weather, people with dogs and children whooping their way up the steps. The tiny shop would be perfect. She was determined to find out more about it.

Despite calls to all the agents in the area she could find no details. Eventually she went to the harbour masters' office to see if he could shed any light on the subject.

"Small shop at the end? She's not for rent," he said. "Can't see the owner letting her out."

"But the shop's empty, paint's peeling. It's in a prime location. Surely it can't be right leaving it empty. Why would anyone do that?"

"Nowt strange about it," the man said. "Sometime there's things more important than money."

Julie sighed. "Well, yes, but it seems such a waste."

He shrugged his shoulders.

Julie sighed again. She wrung her hands in what she hoped was a most appealing way. "Do you know who owns it?" she asked. "Perhaps if I approach them directly…"

"Won't make no difference."

"But I'd like to try." Julie put on her most wheedling voice. "If you tell me who it is…" she stared at him, wide-eyed - brows arched - hopeful.

He chuckled. "It's Adam Trevelyan. His wife had a pottery and pictures shop there. They lived in the flat above. Devastated he were when she died in a boating accident. Shut up shop, moved to the cottage inland so's he couldn't see the sea. Never went back. That's when he joined the lifeboat." He shook his head. "Never been the same since. Shame."

Julie's stomach clenched. She couldn't have been more shocked if he'd punched her. No wonder Adam went so quiet when she talked about her plans to open a jewellery shop. Then she'd asked him if he knew of any premises. He must have thought…

Her face flamed at the memory; how uncaring and stupid she must have seemed, and how insensitive and scheming. No wonder he'd kept his distance.

A few days later she saw him in the boatyard checking a pile of ropes. "Hi," she called. "Lovely morning."

His responding nod appeared welcoming enough so she pressed on. "I owe you an apology," she said, "or an explanation at least."

He glanced up, his face wary.

"I didn't know. Didn't know about the shop, your wife, anything…" She shrugged.

"No reason you should," he said, his voice guarded. He carried on running the rope through his hands.

"I'm sorry, I didn't understand. It's just that the shop is empty. It seems such a waste."

"It's not for rent," he said.

A swell of anxiety swirled in Julie stomach. Suddenly she wanted that shop more than she'd ever wanted anything in her whole life. In her mind it had come to represent everything she'd been working for; a way to make her dreams come true. She persisted. "I realise it must be hard for you what with the memories and everything but it's in a prime location. It would be perfect."

Adam's head shot up. He glared at her. "It's not for rent," he said and threw the rope to the ground before storming away.

Julie sighed. Oh dear, she thought. Now I've upset him again. It was the last thing she'd intended but she'd set her heart on that shop. Thoughts raced through her head. If only she could find a way to make him change his mind.

Christmas with Felicity in London consisted of partying, eating, drinking and various forms of outrageous conduct. Julie told her about Adam's wife.

"He's a lost cause," Felicity said. "He's still in love with his wife. Forget him. There's plenty more fish in the sea."

But Julie couldn't forget him. He kept pushing his way into her thoughts; his easy smile, his grace, his obvious charm. When she sat with her sketch pad doodling her designs she found his face appearing on the page, then she'd have to scribble it out and start again. No one had ever invaded her mind like he did.

Boxing Day evening she was sitting watching TV with Felicity when she saw the report of a trawler being dashed against the rocks in a force ten gale. Lifeboats from around the Cornish coast had been called out. She watched the screen in horror as small boats were tossed like matchsticks on an angry sea. Thirty foot waves lashed the rocks as the crews, in their distinctive yellow oilskins, battled to rescue the trawler-men. There were fears for the lives of two men who had been swept overboard in the storm.

Julie's heart pounded. Alarm surged through her. Supposing Adam was there - of course he would be there – it was what he did. She recalled the harbour master saying he was the bravest coxswain they'd ever had. Reckless even – as though... Sickness swirled inside her at the thoughts running through her brain. She'd never doubted his courage, but to see it there, on the screen in front of her...

She knew she had to get there to be with him.

All the way back thoughts tortured her mind. Don't let it be him... what if... supposing... Trying to rationalise it brought little comfort - he was an experienced sailor, he'd carried out hundreds of rescues... By the time she arrived she was exhausted. A tidal wave of relief flooded over her when she saw lights on in his cottage. Adam was safe. She knocked on his door.

She couldn't hide her joy at seeing him. The warmth of his smile made her heart race. "It's a long time since anyone worried about me," he said. "You'd best come in."

Inside the cottage was warm and welcoming. The room, which had a feminine feel to it, was dominated by the portrait of a woman, whom Julie guessed to be his late wife, in pride of place above the fireplace. Pictures by local artists adorned the other walls; pottery items were dotted around the room on shelves and tables. Julie took a breath. Realisation of the depth of his loss washed over her.

"She was very beautiful," she said.
"She was."

"I'm so sorry. I didn't realise – didn't understand." She swallowed the lump rising in her throat. "You must miss her so much."

He nodded silently, sorrow shadowed his face. "Always," he said.

Julie's heart swelled with remorse.

Adam's gaze moved from the picture to Julie's face. "She would have approved of you," he said. "She would have liked you."

"I'm sure I'd have liked her too," Julie murmured, smiling. She was wearing a necklace from her Hot Chocolate Collection. He touched it, rolling the beads between his fingers.

"She would have loved this. You're very talented." His voice was low and his gaze intense.

Julie blushed. "Thank you," she said. "Perhaps I should stick to designing and give up the idea of the shop."

Adam sighed. "Rachael wouldn't have wanted the shop to stay empty for so long." He gazed at the picture of his late wife. "She loved life, the buzz, the people". He glanced back at Julie. "You can have the shop, the flat too if you want. It's about time I moved on."

Julie gasped. "Do you mean it? Really? I mean…"

"It's what Rachael would have wanted."

Gratitude overwhelmed her. "Thank you, thank you," she said.

His lips twitched into the beginnings of a smile. His face softened and the look in his eyes told Julie all she needed to know.

Her heart pounded. Happiness bubbled up inside her. She'd found everything she'd been looking for right here in the small Cornish fishing village that held so many blissful childhood memories.

He hesitated then she felt him pulling her close. His breath brushed her cheek – and, yes, his lips tasted of salt.

First published in People's Friend in 2013 as 'On the Road to Happiness'

A Treadle to Peddle

"Ow!" Steve grimaced as he banged his knee. "Will this be here much longer?" he said. "I don't mean to be awkward, but it's been months."

Jenny sighed. He was right. Her mum's old treadle standing in their narrow hallway was more than a minor irritation. "I'll get it moved as soon as I can," she said.

She groaned inwardly. It had meant so much to Grace, Jenny's mum, and had been part of her life for more years than anyone cared to remember. Jenny's childhood revolved around her mum's work at the sewing machine, night and day it seemed now. Memories of falling asleep to the soft whirr and rhythmic pounding of the treadle in the next room echoed in her brain. A dressmaker by trade, her mother made all their clothes. She made curtains and sewed shirts and sheets. She even made the rag rug on the floor from cuttings and left over material. Grace and her sewing machine were inextricably linked in Jenny's mind. Still, Steve had a point. In the hall of their modern bungalow it was an eyesore and an obstacle.

"If I can't find a home for it by next week I'll take it down the tip," Jenny assured him, but disappointment churned in her stomach. When Grace moved in with her and Steve they'd had no room to keep much of her stuff, only the small nick-knacks and photos she could keep in her room. All the big stuff had had to go. It was hard enough for her to give up her tiny flat, she'd always been so independent, but they all knew it was for the best. Still, it tore Jenny's heart out to see her mother's life disappearing into the back of the charity shop van. Every item held a precious memory: her favourite armchair, the sideboard where she kept her best china, the everyday crockery, cherished over years. Everything seemed so much part of her. Jenny saw her mum's lips quiver and tears fill her eyes when the men brought out the treadle.

"Can't take that," the driver said. "No market nowadays for old relics."

A look of relief flitted across Grace's face, swift as a dragonfly, but her happiness was short-lived. They both knew it would have to go.

"I'll find a good home for it," Jenny promised, leading her away. "Somewhere it will be appreciated."

Grace smiled gratefully and nodded.

The man at the museum had a kind face. Tall, with a ginger moustache, he reminded Jenny of the young chap who used to call on Mum every couple of weeks, bringing her bundles of work and collecting the finished pieces. Most days she'd be sewing well into the night.

"Just think," she used to say, "My dresses are being sold in the top fashion houses in London." Her face would shine brighter than the sun in August. Jenny felt hopeful.

The man sighed when she explained the reason for her visit. "Just the treadle, you say. No actual sewing machine?"

She shook her head. "The machine was electrified. It went years ago, but Mum kept the treadle." She remembered it, just as it used to be, under the window in Grace's tiny sitting room. She'd kept it covered with an embroidered cloth and her favourite photos stood proudly on it. Some days she just sat in front of it, staring at the world out of her window.

"It's an old friend in a changing world," she used to say.

He shrugged. "Follow me," he said. He took Jenny to a room at the back of the museum. A line of sewing machines, dating from the earliest Singer up to the present day, stood along one wall. "Might have been of interest if you'd had the machine," he said. "But, not just the treadle."

The man in the antique shop wasn't much help either. "Just the base?" he said. "Now, if you had the machine as well..." He raised his eyebrows. "Sorry," he said.

They all squeezed past it for a couple more days, Jenny patting it each time she passed. "Don't worry," she said, "I'll find you a good home," but she was rapidly losing confidence.

The next day Steve came in with two trays of tomato plants for the garden. He struggled to pass the treadle. He didn't say anything, but Jenny saw the flash of annoyance in his eyes when several lumps of soil fell from the trays onto the carpet.

She tried the local retirement home. A nostalgia piece she called it and described the ornate ironwork on the legs and the solid oak top with the hollow for the machine. "Bound to bring back memories for some of your residents," she said, hopefully.

"Might be worth something for the ironwork," Matron said. "Try the scrap yard."

Jenny's face fell and her heart somersaulted in her chest. She imagined the look of horror on her mother's face. She'd wring her hands and tears would fill her eyes.

"No thanks," she said. "I'd rather stick it in the bathroom and sit on it." She couldn't of course: it would never fit.

She wandered the streets for a while, trying to find a solution. Steve was a wonderful, patient man, but he had his limits.

She walked home, full of dread, feeling like she'd let her mum down. "That treadle saved us from starvation," Grace used to say. Jenny's dad died far too young and her mother's work had been their saviour. Her earnings kept the wolf from the door. Her face would soften with affection when she looked at the treadle. Her sentimental attachment was obvious. It was more than wood and metal to her.

Jenny arrived home just as the young man from the garden centre pulled up in his van. "I've got that compost you ordered," he said. "I'll bring it through."

Jenny's heart sank. He'll never get two enormous bales of compost past the obstacle in the hall, she thought.

She thought wrong. He hoisted the first bag onto his shoulder and strode up the path, leaving her in his wake.

"Wow," he said when he saw the treadle. He swung the bale of compost onto the floor and crouched down gazing at it. He ran his hands over the ironwork and inspected the still intact leather belt. "How fantastic," he said. "Just the thing for the garden." His eyes shone like fairy lights.

"The garden?" Jenny said, puzzled.

"Yes. Paint it white and put plants in the hollow where the machine used to be." He grinned. "Make a great talking point," he said.

He was right. The treadle looked a treat standing under the kitchen window, brimming with Grace's favourite red geraniums. That summer Jenny sat with her mum on the patio, sipping tea. She couldn't help but smile when she saw the twinkle of pleasure in Grace's cornflower blue eyes.

"I'm glad you found a home for it," Grace said. "Moving in with you was difficult enough without giving up all my treasures."

First published in The Weekly News in 2011

Something Lost

I watched the young couple walking down the street, their arms around each other. She gazed lovingly into his eyes and he gave her a squeeze. That used to be us, I thought, Harry and me. I sighed.

"There's something missing, I'm not sure what it is, but I want it back," I said. I was with my friend, Lyn in the coffee shop in town for our regular weekly gripe and moan session, putting the world to rights.

"When we were first married Harry never left me without giving me a kiss, he bought me flowers every week and held my hand in the street, so proud he was to be seen with me." I took a sip of coffee and grimaced. "Nowadays I might as well be invisible, it's as if the closeness has gone, drowned in a sea of worries, children and growing old."

"You can't expect love's young bloom to last forever," Lyn said. "My Barry spends all his time in the shed and he talks to the plants in the greenhouse more than he talks to me. Men…who'd have 'em?"

Well, me, I thought. I would. I sighed. "Harry's lovely and I wouldn't swap him for the world, but I wish he'd be a bit more…you know…attentive. Sometimes I feel like a piece of furniture that's been there so long you stop noticing it."

Lyn gazed at me and smiled. "I know what you mean. When I first married Barry, we were so close I knew what he was thinking. I could finish a sentence before he said it. Now…" She shrugged.

We sat in silence for a while, pondering over our coffee. "What about a weekend break," she said, brightening. "Book a nice hotel somewhere romantic and spring it on him as a surprise. That should put the sparkle back."

I thought about it and warmed to the idea; then reality set in. I shook my head. "There's nothing I'd like better," I said. "A posh hotel, waited on hand and foot, pampered and fussed over - perfect, but Harry would hate it. His idea of a great weekend is camping out on a riverbank, spending all day fishing and all evening in the pub watching football. No, it's no good unless it's something we'd both enjoy. It'd cost a fortune and Harry would say it's a waste of money."

Lyn sighed. "Barry would never leave his tomatoes this time of year and I'd never be able to drag him away from the allotment either, so I understand the problem. Men! They're hopeless."

"Well, not entirely," I said with a grin. "My Harry's good at some things."

The following week, sitting in the same coffee shop in town, Lyn produced a magazine from her eco-friendly bag-for-life. "Look at this," she said, shoving it in my face.

A full-page spread featured a glamorous model in a soft-focus pose. It read: 'Unleash your inner glamour and take a walk on the wild side'. Then it went on to promise that, with their expert guidance, anyone could look a million dollars.

Experienced stylists offered hair, make-up, manicure and fashion advice to turn the most ordinary into something exotic and enthralling. There was also a photo session with a professional photographer and one free photo. I took a deep breath. If I looked half as good as the model it would certainly make Harry sit up and take notice, but could I? Would I? Dare I?

"I don't know what to say," I said eventually to Lyn.

"It's easy," she said. "Say yes. What could it hurt?"

"Apart from the fifty quid?" I said.

"There's a special offer – two for the price of one. We could both go. It's coming up to your birthday, why don't we do it as a treat?" The grin on her face spread from ear to ear. "Come on, it'll be fun and you did want to re-ignite that spark."

Lyn was right; I deserved a birthday treat, so we booked it.

The girl on the telephone asked what kind of look we were aiming for. "Something guaranteed to knock our husbands' eyes out," Lyn said. She laughed and suggested we find pictures of what we had in mind and they'd do their best to match it.

The next day Lyn came over and we spent the afternoon going through my stack of magazines, and each chose a picture of our preferred role model. I chose Meryl Streep in *Mamma Mia* and Lyn chose Cheryl Cole.

"We might as well make it as challenging as we can," Lyn said, laughing.

The brochure said to bring a selection of outfits and accessories, so the day before the session Lyn brought her stuff round, I turned out my wardrobe, jewellery box and accessories drawer and we spent a hilarious afternoon choosing our outfits. It reminded me of diving into the dressing up box when we were kids and the fun we used to have. At least that's one thing we haven't lost, I thought, our sense of humour.

The first item I tried on was the suit I had worn to my daughter's summer wedding. Lyn shook her head. "That's 'Ladies' Day at Ascot'," she said. "We're looking for 'night-time in Paris'."

I giggled. I didn't have anything that remotely resembled a night out in Paris. "I'm aiming to stun with simple sophistication," I said, "not knock Harry unconscious with a front row seat at the Folies Bergere."

Lyn insisted we'd need bright colours for dramatic effect, so back went my beiges, camels and pastels and out came my sparkly evening outfits; anything, shimmery, low cut or revealing.

I tried on Lyn's midnight blue Grecian top with its softly draped neckline edged with silver that highlighted the creaminess of my ample bosom. The colour brought out the sapphire in my eyes. It looked fabulous.

Next I put in a white silk camisole to wear under my crimson velvet jacket and a deep purple top that I'd bought on a mad impulse in the sales and never worn. I also threw in my staple little black dress for good measure, a long black skirt and some evening trousers.

Lyn looked fantastic in my shimmery, bottle green dress that fitted where it touched, the colour reflecting the emerald in her eyes. She added a couple of her dressier numbers for luck. We paraded up and down in front of the mirror like a couple of teenagers let loose in a clothing store. If nothing else, we had a lot of fun.

Accessories were easier. I had an unbelievable array of scarves ranging from pale to gaudy and had no problem picking half-a-dozen, mostly chiffon and floaty.

We spent hours going through my jewellery boxes, trying everything on. I discovered things hidden at the bottom of the box that hadn't seen the light of day for years. Every piece brought back a precious memory.

Rooting through my jewellery was an enjoyable pastime, but it didn't bring us any nearer to deciding what to take. I sighed. Gold and bold was the way to go, so that's what we did, although I did include a row of pearls that held a special memory. I added a huge Victorian ring picked up in a flea market and diamond and pearl drop-earrings.

The day of the session dawned bright and clear. The freshness of the perfect spring day boded well. Flowers bursting into bloom and new life sprouting from the trees felt like a good omen as we caught the train to town.

The salon was luxurious, I felt a little overawed, but Lyn barged right in. The receptionist was charming, took our coats and ushered us into a dimly lit room with soft music playing for our 'personal consultations' which included generous helpings of complimentary champagne.

The day went so quickly I can hardly recall the details although I do remember the feeling of indulgence. I also recall sinking back in a massage chair to have my hair shampooed. A most peculiar feeling at first but I soon came to enjoy it. I made a mental note to mention it to Maureen, my regular hairdresser, not that she'd go in for such extravagance.

I asked Raoul, the hairstylist, who looked about fifteen, "How long have your been doing this sort of thing?"

"About eighteen years," he said. "I've worked all over the world, once on a cruise ship and on a film set. This is the best though, helping beautiful women make the most of themselves." He was so nice I relaxed as he snipped, brushed, highlighted, curled, teased, and sprayed my straw-like thatch.

Lyn had copper highlights put in her rich chestnut locks, swept up in soft curls onto the top of her head. "Great hair," I said when her stylist had finished. "Shame about the face."

We both collapsed in champagne-fuelled laughter as we made our way through to the make-up room.

"What's that stuff they use to fill in the cracks on the wall?" Lyn asked. "We could do with a bucket-load in here." I managed to stifle my giggles.

The girl in make-up was lovely and so dedicated I allowed her free reign to practice her artistry on my face. She smoothed, patted and painted. "Lavender eye-shadow and blusher to bring out your eyes," she said. I nodded and smiled. By the end of the session, I had enough make-up on to plaster the living room wall.

"Of course it has to be thick for the photo," Lyn said, as she posed this way and that in the mirror next to me. "You wouldn't put this much on at home."

Next stop was the manicurist. I chose a pale pink varnish. The young Chinese girl shook her head. She selected a deep plum polish. I swallowed back my comment about dark colours showing the chips, reminding myself that glamour models don't have to worry about chipped nail varnish. They don't have to wash up either, I thought, but said nothing. Lyn chose vivid scarlet.

The last thing was the photographer. We had our pictures taken separately and together in various positions. There was even one of me giving come-hither looks while swinging in a flower-bedecked hammock. I almost fell out and had Lyn creasing up with laughter. I hadn't had so much fun in ages and the time flew by faster than an express train on speed.

There was a special viewing room for us to see the photos, accompanied by more champagne. I'd expected more of a transformation. The photographer must have notice my disappointment.

"What's wrong?" he asked.

I sighed. "I thought I'd look fabulous," I said, "but I've still got eye-bags and more wrinkles than a ten-year-old russet apple."

He laughed. Then he did something magical with his mouse thing and the eye-bags, wrinkles and sagging jaw-line all disappeared.

"Now do it for real," Lyn said. One consolation was that Lyn still looked like Lyn, only done up like a dog's dinner. Cheryl Cole had nothing to worry about.

We each chose our free photo and bought one of the two of us together as a souvenir.

On the way home I gazed in wonderment at my photo. "If only," I said. "If only I looked like that. Still, I've had a great time and it's been an experience I'll never forget."

"Me neither," Lyn said. "I wonder what Harry will say when he meets us at the station."

Harry! I'd quite forgotten the reason for our day out. "I bet he doesn't even notice," I said, coming rapidly back to earth.

"Of course he will. You wait, he'll be amazed."

I wished I could believe it.

By the time we arrived at the station it had started to rain, a light drizzle that sunk my spirits even further. I stood in the station, looking glum. "I don't have an umbrella," I said. "My hair will flop and my make up will run and I'll look such a fright that Harry will think I've escaped from a Halloween horror movie."

Lyn sighed. "You're an old worry wort. It won't be like that at all."

Then I saw Harry running along the pavement. He ran up to Lyn. "Come on quick," he said. "I'm parked on a double yellow." He looked right past me.

Lyn hesitated. Harry did a double take. "What have you done to my Izzie?" he said, looking straight at me. "Where is she?"

"It's me." I said. "The new improved Izzie, glamorous and alluring." I fluttered my newly extended eyelashes.

His face crumpled. "There was nowt wrong with t'old Izzie," he said, in his gruffest Yorkshire tone. A frown creased his brow. My heart sank faster than a rock in quicksand.

Then a sly smile spread across his face and a twinkle lit up his amber eyes. He rubbed his hands together. "Still," he said, "a change might be a challenge."

The look in his eye told me all I needed to know. Excitement fizzed through me like bubbles in champagne. I felt the old loving spark between us that I'd missed for so long. It wasn't lost after all.

First published in People's Friend Annual 2013

Easy Pickings

Summer in London, hot, steamy and teeming with tourists. They're everywhere, filling the streets, cafés, bars and restaurants, bringing their colourful vibrancy to the city.

I stand on the steps by Westminster Bridge watching the stream of bodies snaking endlessly across to South Bank. They come in all shapes and sizes, old ladies in coats, young lads in shorts and giggling girls wearing hardly anything at all.

Every nation in the world is represented here: Asians, Europeans, Americans, Africans, all adding to the cosmopolitan melting pot that is London.

Tourist guides hold their striped, furled umbrellas high as they stride purposefully forward, like Moses leading the Israelites through the Red Sea.

On rainy days the umbrellas are open and held high. The bridge becomes a pageant of colour with umbrellas vying for space on the crowded pavement. Today the sun sparkles on the water and gilds the windows of the buildings along the riverside.

The guides are followed by a raggle-taggle of weary sight-seers eager to cram in yet more history and an over-indulgence of culture. Some are anxious to get on while others would tarry to enjoy the view, thrilled at just being here. An abundance of cameras, smart phones and tablets are on show to record scenes viewed through lenses that reduce the city's splendid opulence to bite size pieces, losing its magnificence in the process. Easy pickings.

I pick out the vulnerable ones, the elderly and frail, the young and naïve, the unaware and unsuspecting in the hustle and bustle of London as she puts on her glamour, glitz and shine to woo the visitors.

Over the bridge I watch boats bobbing against the pier offering the chance to cruise a river older than the

dawn of time. Music drifts up from the steel band below mingling with the aroma of candy-floss and fried onions. The atmosphere is one of lively noise and confusion. Easy pickings for some.

There's a few of us out by the river today. I don't work alone. I'm the spotter. It's my job to identify the possible victims. I'm good at my job. I work out my best choices for easy pickings: pick-pocketing, snatch and grab, the please help me con. It's amazing how many old ladies and gentlemen will get out their purses to help an innocent-looking young person if approached. No one is safe. All should be on their guard, but few are.

I spot an old lady, oblivious to her surroundings, handbag hooked loosely over her arm as she cranes her neck to take a photo of Big Ben. How difficult would it be to snatch that bag? How worthwhile? Hmm. The elderly can be quite tenacious. They are not easily overcome.

Along South Bank people dawdle, stopping and staring at the street artists, statues, and entertainments. Easier pickings.

A young girl walks down the steps on the south side of the bridge. She's completely engrossed in a technological world of her own, focussed only on the screen on her phone – probably taking pictures no one will ever see. She's wearing red hot pants, a sleeveless crop top and flip-flop – no good for running after an assailant. Her long skinny legs are brown from the sun and her blonde hair is tied back. Her headphones isolate her from the world around her.

Does she know where she is? Does she even care? She's brought her world with her and it's not allowing her to become part of ours. Will it be her today?

The stream of bodies moving along South Bank slows as they approach the London Eye. Crowds have gathered at the entrance to the attraction.

Experience tells me this would be the perfect place.

Sure enough I see him, a lad on a skateboard weaving his way through the crowds, just another youngster out enjoying the sun? I text my contacts, we work as a team. We've been together for years now – very successfully.

Within seconds he runs into the oblivious girl, knocking her off balance and grabbing her phone. Then he's away, skating through the crowds before she even has time to realise what has happened to her. It's quick; no one is ever quite prepared for the speed of it. She's stunned and paralysed with shock.

The lad races away, a grin on his face. The grin disappears as he sails straight into the arms of my waiting colleagues, PC Nick Brown and PC Earnest White. I imagine the smiles on their faces as they give the time-honoured greeting, "You're nicked son."

He'll be in Court in the morning. No defence. I've caught it all on camera. London will be a tiny bit safer today. No easy pickings while we're around.

I scan the crowd crossing the bridge. Who's next I wonder?

*First published on the Internet on
www.londonist.com in 2014*

You Can See France from Here

"I've lost the use of my legs, not my frigging brain," Father yelled, his bony fingers snatching the keys from the desk. Propelling himself towards the corridor in the direction of our rooms, he yelled at me, "Come on Betty, move your fat arse."

My heart sank even as the colour rose to my cheeks. Mouthing a silent "Sorry" to the receptionist, I picked up our suitcases and staggered after him. Jeez, I thought, what on earth sort of holiday is this going to be? I already knew the answer.

"I'll bang on the wall when I want you," he said, swinging his chair round as I put his case on the bed.

"I'll pop back in half-an-hour," I said, not wanting him to call the shots on our first day.

"What a shit-hole," he said. "I've seen more comfortable doss-houses."

I shook my head and retreated. I had lived all my life in fear of my father. Meanness shrouded him like a cloak and spitefulness came more natural to him than breathing. The phone call from the nursing home, where he had lived since my mother died, well, more accurately, gave up living, had not come as any surprise to me.

"You'll have to make other arrangements," Matron told me. "We've given him plenty of warnings and second-chances, but as you know the majority of our staff are from ethnic minorities. We have to take racial abuse very seriously. I'm afraid he'll have to go."

Despair rose inside me. "He's an old man," I said. "Can't you make some suitable arrangements for him?"

"I'm sorry. He's upset the other residents too. We can't have him here any longer. He's been threatening physical violence."

"He's an old man in a wheel-chair," I said. "Surely no one takes his threats seriously?"

"Perhaps he could come and stay with you…"

I shuddered at the thought. Of course she was right. If anyone, seeing the wheelchair, thought him frail they were in for a rude awakening. Arthritis may have crippled him but it had not lessened his power to put the fear of God into anyone who displeased him.

"It may take some time," I said, meekly.

"End of the week," she said, and put the phone down. Hence the holiday on the Isle of Wight. I thought it would at least give me time to make other arrangements for him.

"It will be an adventure," I told him. "A chance to re-visit the places where you spent your childhood."

"An adventure? Well, anything's got to better than stagnating in this smelly rat-hole," he said. So I booked us into The Lobster Pot. A small hotel on the front at Sandown.

My heart lifted when I saw the hotel. It looked warm and welcoming. Colourful hanging baskets, overflowing with pink and red geraniums, adorned the white-washed walls. Half-barrel planters on the terraces brimmed with ballerina fuschias and pelagoniums and on the blue-painted window sills, boxes of bright pink begonias beamed at us. The overall effect was a symphony of red, white and blue.

The smell of roasting meat greeted us as we entered, bringing a rush of saliva to my mouth. If the cooking smells were anything to go by at least we'd be well fed.

Dinner on the first night went without incident and I began to think that perhaps he'd mellowed over the years. Perhaps, if it came to it, I could have him at home with me. I lived alone, Mum had managed him, why shouldn't I? My cheerful optimism didn't last long.

Every morning, as the pale sunlight crept over the windowsill in the small dining room, he'd manoeuvre his chair to block the gangway. Then he'd make a big fuss as people tried to squeeze past. I saw the flash of satisfaction in his eyes as people offered their apologies. I cringed as he loudly criticised whatever was put in front of him, pushing the plate away, like a petulant child. I'm not sure what was most embarrassing, watching him eat or listening to him whining that it was inedible.

Once we got outside things improved. I pushed him along the promenade, overlooking the bay.

"We used to come here every year when I was a child," he said, with a smile, so rare I didn't recognise it. "Did I tell you how I won the raft race every year, youngest competitor too? And I could out swim boys much older than me. Outrun them too."

I had heard all his stories and grown up with his exploits even as they had grown over the years, expanding with every telling. Now, I thought, he had little left but the memories.

"Course it's all different now," he said. "Milk-sops and mummy's boys, computer games and television. No spirit of adventure, young lads today. Not like in our day. My dad used to beat me with a strap. Wouldn't do these kids any harm to feel a bit of leather across their back-sides."

The first three days the weather disappointed, with pearl grey skies threatening rain. Still, every day I drove out to one of the resort towns, parked and settled him in

145

his chair for long bracing walks along the sea-front promenades.

My hands weren't as nimble as they used to be. "Stop fussing woman," he'd say as I wrapped a blanket over his legs and pulled a woolly hat over his sparse grey hair. Then he'd take a warming swig from his silver hip flask. Things generally improved after that.

I'd pull my coat close around me, but the cold wind bit through, fluttering my head-scarf and stinging my face. My hands numbed, turning blue as I pushed the chair against the bitter blast and my eyes watered, but he was impervious to my discomfort. I'd gaze enviously at the holidaymakers huddled in the warmth of their cars parked on the front.

"You don't get enough good fresh air," he said, his cruel eyes dancing with mirth. "Gone soft, that's your trouble."

On the fourth day the weather improved and our walks became more enjoyable. He talked about his holidays as a child, running down to the beach every day, chasing butterflies and calling to seagulls as they swooped and dived for the bread he threw for them a long time ago under a summer sky. Sailing, rafting and canoeing, he re-lived them all, the toughest and bravest adventurer on the sea. But after a while the reminiscences only served to remind him of his deteriorating condition and the meanness returned.

"Changed beyond recognition," he moaned. "Trashy commercialism and opportunistic rubbish," he'd say as we walked along past amusement arcades, with their flashing neon lights and the constant crash of money dropping through the slot machines. The smell of hot-dogs and onions mingled with doughnuts and candyfloss and I wished we could stop just for a while to breathe in the lively vibrant atmosphere. I loved the hurdy-gurdy music of the rides and the calls of the stall-holders and bingo-callers. If only things were different, I thought, what a lovely holiday we could have.

"Shit-holes. Every-where's turned into a shit-hole," he'd announce and my stomach would curl in turmoil lest I incur his further displeasure by tarrying too long. He wasn't above using his cane to hurry me along.

We stopped in a small café in Ryde for a cup of tea. I wheeled him to a window where he could look out and watch the sailboats. At the counter, waiting to be served, I recognised the man stood in front of me. A bear of a man with silver grey hair and a matching beard, he turned and smiled as I joined the queue behind him. Early fifties but fit he was. I bet he works out, I thought.

"Hi, you're staying at the Lobster Pot too, aren't you? How are you enjoying your holiday?"

"Better now the weather's improved," I said, mortified at the memory of his daily embarrassment trying to squeeze past Father's wheelchair.

"My name's Jim, Jim Baxter." He held out his hand.

His hand enveloped mine, soft warmth spread through me like melting butter. My heart raced. "Betty," I said. "Betty Carraway."

"Your father is it?" He nodded towards the window where father sat glaring at us.

I nodded, unable to summon my voice from its hiding place.

"Look, there's a quiz night in the bar tonight, if you're interested. Why not join us?" I couldn't help but notice how tanned his face was and the way his blue eyes twinkled.

"I'm not sure Father would…"

"I'm not asking your father. Not joined at the hip are you?" The soft country burr in his voice made my heart quiver.

I laughed. "Thankfully no," I said. "I'll see what I can do."

"Good," he said.

Father became surly after the tea incident. Nothing pleased him. Later, when I mentioned the quiz night he flew into a rage. "Don't be so blooming ridiculous," he said. "Making a fool of yourself at your age." Then he developed chest pains and insisted that I sit with him, reading to him to calm his shattered nerves. "Not that you give a damn," he sneered accusingly. "Things will be different when I come to live with you," he said. "There'll have to be changes."

On our last day we went to St. Catherine's point. The sun shone and the day was warm.

"You can see France from here," Father said, as we drove into the car park at the bottom of a steep hill. I manhandled him into his chair, making sure he wore his cap against the sun, then I pushed him up to the front where we stopped to look out across the English Channel.

I could see the beach and the foot of the cliffs where the sea eddied and flowed into rock pools filled with seaweed and children netting crabs.

Families played on the beach in the bright sunshine, laughing and splashing in the rolling waves, jumping over the white foam as it broke against the shore. It looked so happy and normal that I felt a pang of regret, my chest heaving for what might have been.

"Can't see France from here stupid. Get us up to the top of the hill."

I turned the chair and pushed it across the car park. Just as I was taking a breath, ready to begin the long slog up the hill, I felt a presence at my side. It was Jim, materialised from nowhere, carrying a rucksack.

"Can I help?" he said.

"No you can sod off," Father replied. "She can manage."

Jim laughed, his gaze travelling appreciatively over my ample frame. His lips parted in a grin exposing perfect white teeth. A tingle ran down my spine.

"It's no trouble," he said and pushed the chair quickly up the hill as if it was nothing at all. He was wearing khaki shorts and light brown walking boots and I stared wistfully at the hairs on his muscular, tanned legs, turned golden by the sun.

At the top of the hill he swung the chair onto a concrete plinth marking the viewpoint. "Glorious view," he said looking straight into my eyes.

The breeze tousled his hair. He held my gaze far longer than was prudent. I felt my skin reddening.

"Can't see a bloody thing," Father said.

Reluctantly, I turned to look out across the sea. "Over there, isn't that it?" I pointed at a slight darkening on the horizon.

"Don't be so bloody daft woman, there's nothing there."

Irritation rose inside me at the sound of Father's voice. If it hadn't been for the pounding in my ears I'd have sworn that my heart had stopped beating.

Jim shook his head. "Well, I'll love you and leave you," he said. "Have a nice day. Might see you later?"

His eyebrows rose and I nodded, holding my breath in case Father saw, but he was fiddling in his blanket, searching for his binoculars.

Jim squeezed my arm before turning away and striding out along the black tarmac that snaked its way across the fields.

"Bloody waste of time," Father said, scanning the horizon with his binoculars. "Can't see sod all."

The sun broke out from behind a cloud as I swung the chair onto the road, facing back the way we had come. It warmed my face.

At the top of the incline the chair slipped from my grasp. I stood, rooted to the spot as it started its decent, rapidly gathering speed. It was half-way down when he must have realised his solitary state.

He started waving his arms in the air, but any protest he made was lost in the breeze that rustled through the long grass, until he met the lorry that was coming around the bend at the bottom of the hill.

Thus he started on his greatest adventure and I started on mine.

First published on The Strictly Writing site in November 2010

If you have enjoyed these stories you may also enjoy Kay's novels:

The Guardian Angel

When Nell Draper leaves the workhouse to care for the five-year-old son of Lord Eversham, she has no idea of the heartache that lies ahead of her.

Robert can't speak. He can't tell her what makes him happy or sad. Nell has to work that out for herself.

Not everyone is happy about Robert's existence.

Can Nell save him from a desolate future, secure his inheritance and ensure he takes his rightful place in society?

A love story.

Reader Review:

This is a very complicated story, so many things are going on. There is murder, stealing, supposed kidnapping and deceit. The characters are so true to life and the descriptions and dialogue are spot on. The author has spun all the threads together to make one heck of a good tale. I read it in one sitting, it kept me so enthralled. I love the interaction between the boy and his care giver. She protected him, loved and educated him, to the best of her ability. (Cindy Briggs)

The Water Gypsy

When Tilly Thompson, a girl from the canal, is caught stealing a pie from the terrace of The Imperial Hotel, Athelstone, the intervention of Captain Charles Thackery saves her from prison.

The Captain's favour stirs up jealously and hatred among the hotel staff, especially Freddie, the stable boy who harbours desires of his own.

Freddie's pursuit leads Tilly into far greater danger than she could ever have imagined. Can she escape the prejudice, persecution and hypocrisy of Victorian Society, leave her past behind and find true happiness?

This is a story of love and loss, lust and passion, injustice and ultimate redemption.

The Water Gypsy was a finalist in The Wishing Shelf 2014 Award

Praise for The Water Gypsy:

I thoroughly enjoyed reading 'The Water Gypsy'. It deals with prejudice and poverty, injustice and exploitation but it is done in such a subtle and thoughtful way that it does not detract from a gripping story line with compelling characters. The best thing about it was that I had no idea what would happen next! I look forward to more writing from this author. **Penny Duggan** (author and historian).

The Watercress Girls

Spirited and beautiful Annie Flanagan's reckless ambition takes her from the Hackney watercress beds to dancing at the Folies-Bergère in Paris. She returns to work in an establishment catering to the needs of wealthy and influential gentlemen.

When she disappears, leaving her illegitimate son behind, her friend Hettie Bundy sets out to find her. Hettie's search leads her from the East End of London, where opium dens and street gangs rule, to uncover the corruption and depravity in Victorian society.

Secrets are revealed that put both girls' lives in danger. Can Hettie find Annie in time? What does the future hold for the watercress girls?

A Victorian Mystery

The Watercress Girls was chosen as a finalist in The Wishing Shelf Awards 2015

5* Reviews:

Congratulations Kay on a really excellent second novel! It is a real page-turner from the first pages to the last. Not only is it filled with suspense - a real page-turner - the novel successfully captures the spirit of the Victorian age; and it is easy to warm to the believable characters. I really enjoyed 'The Watercress Girls' and look forward to reading more novels by Kay Seeley. (Barbara Towell)

Another excellent read from this author. I used to live round the London Docks so this was particularly interesting to me. I loved the moments in the Docks and the book is very well researched. The characters are strong and unique and you root for them to succeed (and find that special someone!) The information on the watercress sellers was very interesting as I had not heard of this aspect of London's history before. Can't wait for the next book from this author, in the meantime I will re-read this one! (Lillibook)

I loved Kay's Water Gypsy and eagerly awaited her new book. The wait was worthwhile. Fabulous book couldn't put it down. Finished it in three evenings. Well written excellent story line. Thank you Kay for a really interesting book. Look forward to your next one. (Jill Clegg)

Please feel free to contact Kay through her website www.kayseeleyauthor.com

She'd love to hear from you.

Lightning Source UK Ltd.
Milton Keynes UK
UKHW020340240819
348481UK00015B/1282/P